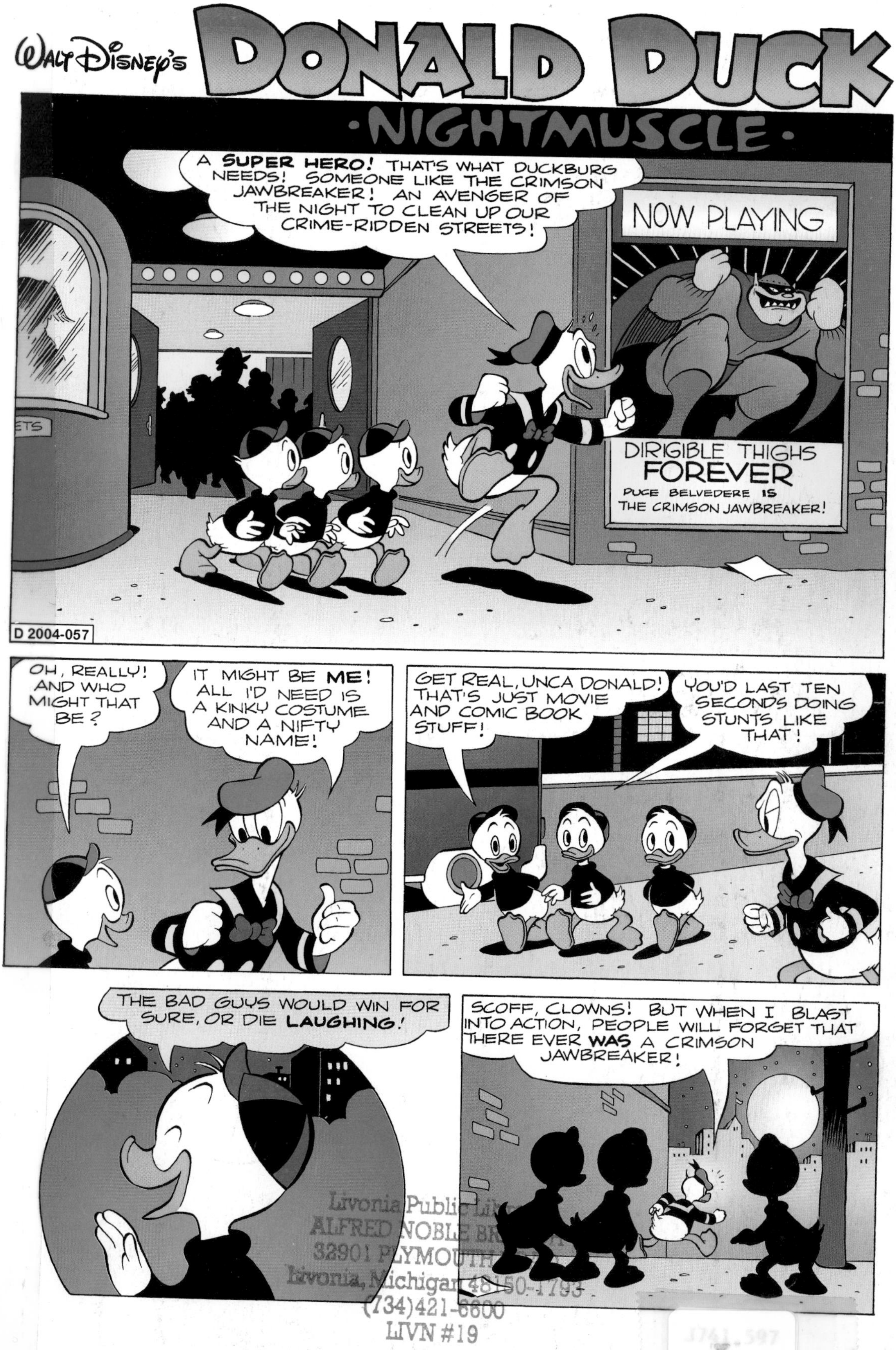

Walt Disney's
DONALD DUCK
·NIGHTMUSCLE·
A SUPER HERO! THAT'S WHAT DUCKBURG NEEDS! SOMEONE LIKE THE CRIMSON JAWBREAKER! AN AVENGER OF THE NIGHT TO CLEAN UP OUR CRIME-RIDDEN STREETS!
NOW PLAYING
DIRIGIBLE THIGHS FOREVER
PUCE BELVEDERE IS THE CRIMSON JAWBREAKER!
ETS
D 2004-057
OH, REALLY! AND WHO MIGHT THAT BE?
IT MIGHT BE ME! ALL I'D NEED IS A KINKY COSTUME AND A NIFTY NAME!
GET REAL, UNCA DONALD! THAT'S JUST MOVIE AND COMIC BOOK STUFF!
YOU'D LAST TEN SECONDS DOING STUNTS LIKE THAT!
THE BAD GUYS WOULD WIN FOR SURE, OR DIE LAUGHING!
SCOFF, CLOWNS! BUT WHEN I BLAST INTO ACTION, PEOPLE WILL FORGET THAT THERE EVER WAS A CRIMSON JAWBREAKER!

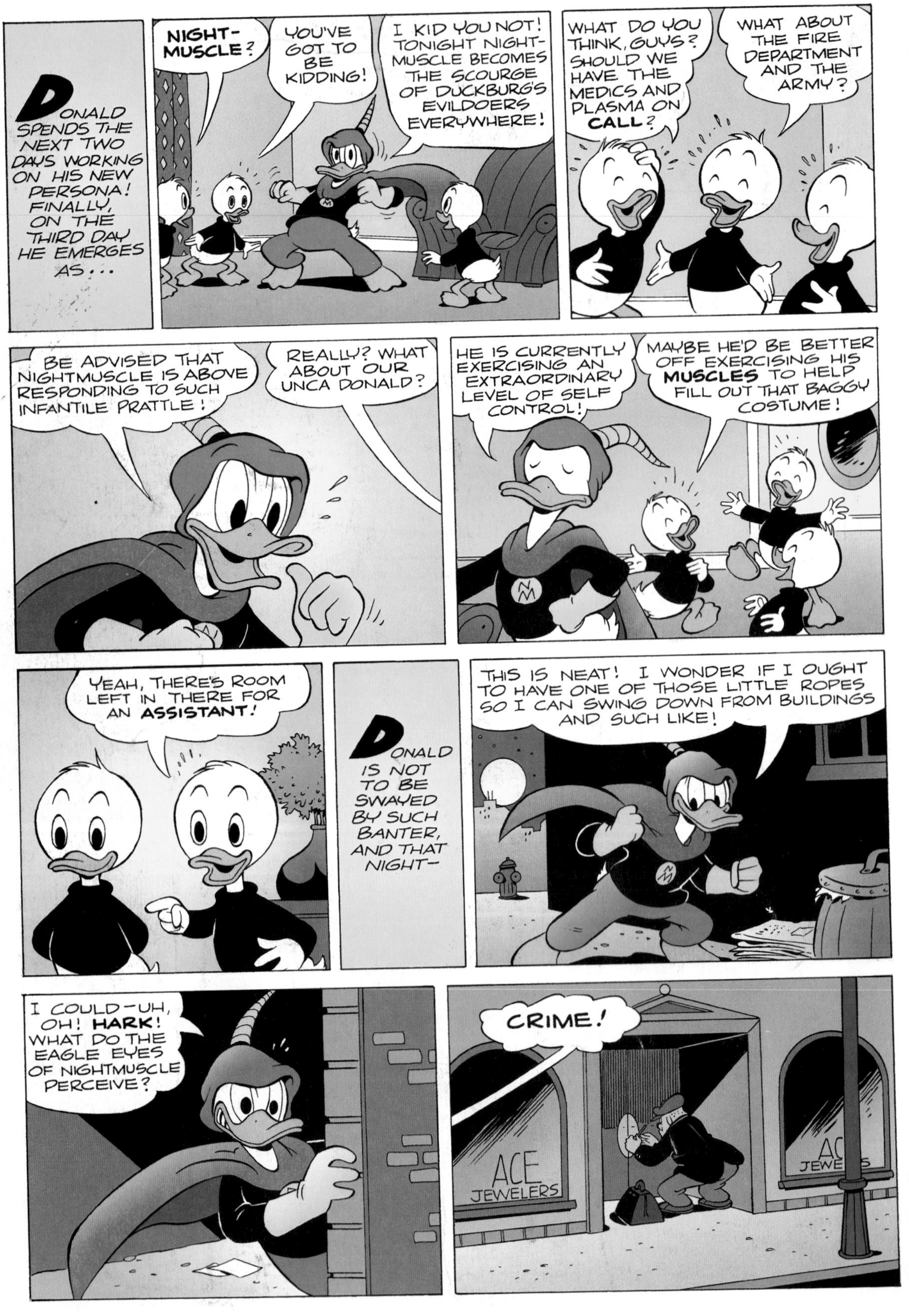
DONALD SPENDS THE NEXT TWO DAYS WORKING ON HIS NEW PERSONA! FINALLY, ON THE THIRD DAY HE EMERGES AS...
NIGHT-MUSCLE?
YOU'VE GOT TO BE KIDDING!
I KID YOU NOT! TONIGHT NIGHT-MUSCLE BECOMES THE SCOURGE OF DUCKBURG'S EVILDOERS EVERYWHERE!
WHAT DO YOU THINK, GUYS? SHOULD WE HAVE THE MEDICS AND PLASMA ON CALL?
WHAT ABOUT THE FIRE DEPARTMENT AND THE ARMY?
BE ADVISED THAT NIGHTMUSCLE IS ABOVE RESPONDING TO SUCH INFANTILE PRATTLE!
REALLY? WHAT ABOUT OUR UNCA DONALD?
HE IS CURRENTLY EXERCISING AN EXTRAORDINARY LEVEL OF SELF CONTROL!
MAYBE HE'D BE BETTER OFF EXERCISING HIS MUSCLES TO HELP FILL OUT THAT BAGGY COSTUME!
YEAH, THERE'S ROOM LEFT IN THERE FOR AN ASSISTANT!
DONALD IS NOT TO BE SWAYED BY SUCH BANTER, AND THAT NIGHT—
THIS IS NEAT! I WONDER IF I OUGHT TO HAVE ONE OF THOSE LITTLE ROPES SO I CAN SWING DOWN FROM BUILDINGS AND SUCH LIKE!
I COULD—UH, OH! HARK! WHAT DO THE EAGLE EYES OF NIGHTMUSCLE PERCEIVE?
CRIME!
ACE JEWELERS

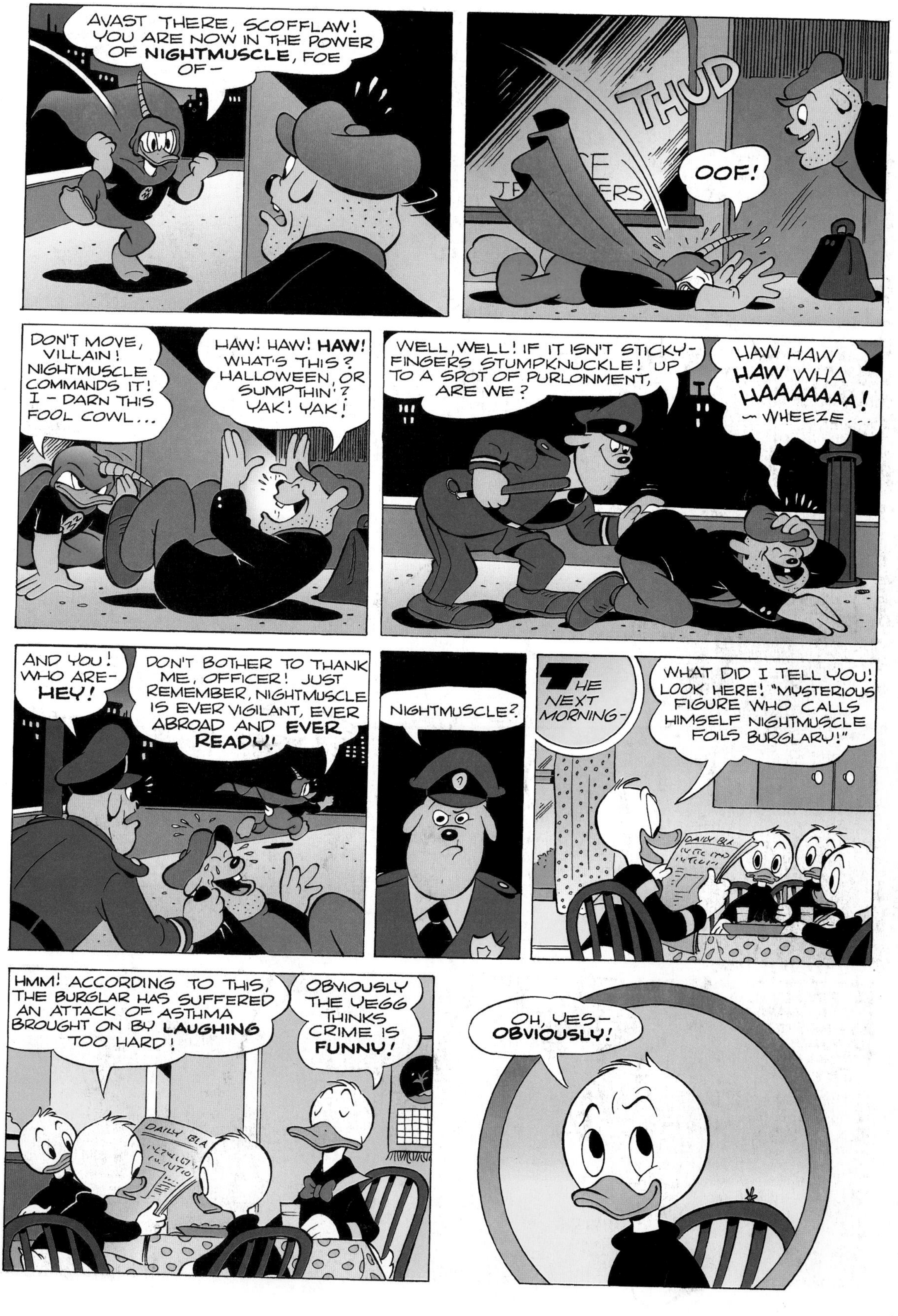
AVAST THERE, SCOFFLAW! YOU ARE NOW IN THE POWER OF NIGHTMUSCLE, FOE OF –
THUD
OOF!
DON'T MOVE, VILLAIN! NIGHTMUSCLE COMMANDS IT! I – DARN THIS FOOL COWL...
HAW! HAW! HAW! WHAT'S THIS? HALLOWEEN, OR SUMPTHIN'? YAK! YAK!
WELL, WELL! IF IT ISN'T STICKY-FINGERS STUMPKNUCKLE! UP TO A SPOT OF PURLOINMENT, ARE WE?
HAW HAW HAW WHA HAAAAAAA! ~ WHEEZE...
AND YOU! WHO ARE– HEY!
DON'T BOTHER TO THANK ME, OFFICER! JUST REMEMBER, NIGHTMUSCLE IS EVER VIGILANT, EVER ABROAD AND EVER READY!
NIGHTMUSCLE?
THE NEXT MORNING–
WHAT DID I TELL YOU! LOOK HERE! "MYSTERIOUS FIGURE WHO CALLS HIMSELF NIGHTMUSCLE FOILS BURGLARY!"
HMM! ACCORDING TO THIS, THE BURGLAR HAS SUFFERED AN ATTACK OF ASTHMA BROUGHT ON BY LAUGHING TOO HARD!
OBVIOUSLY THE YEGG THINKS CRIME IS FUNNY!
OH, YES– OBVIOUSLY!

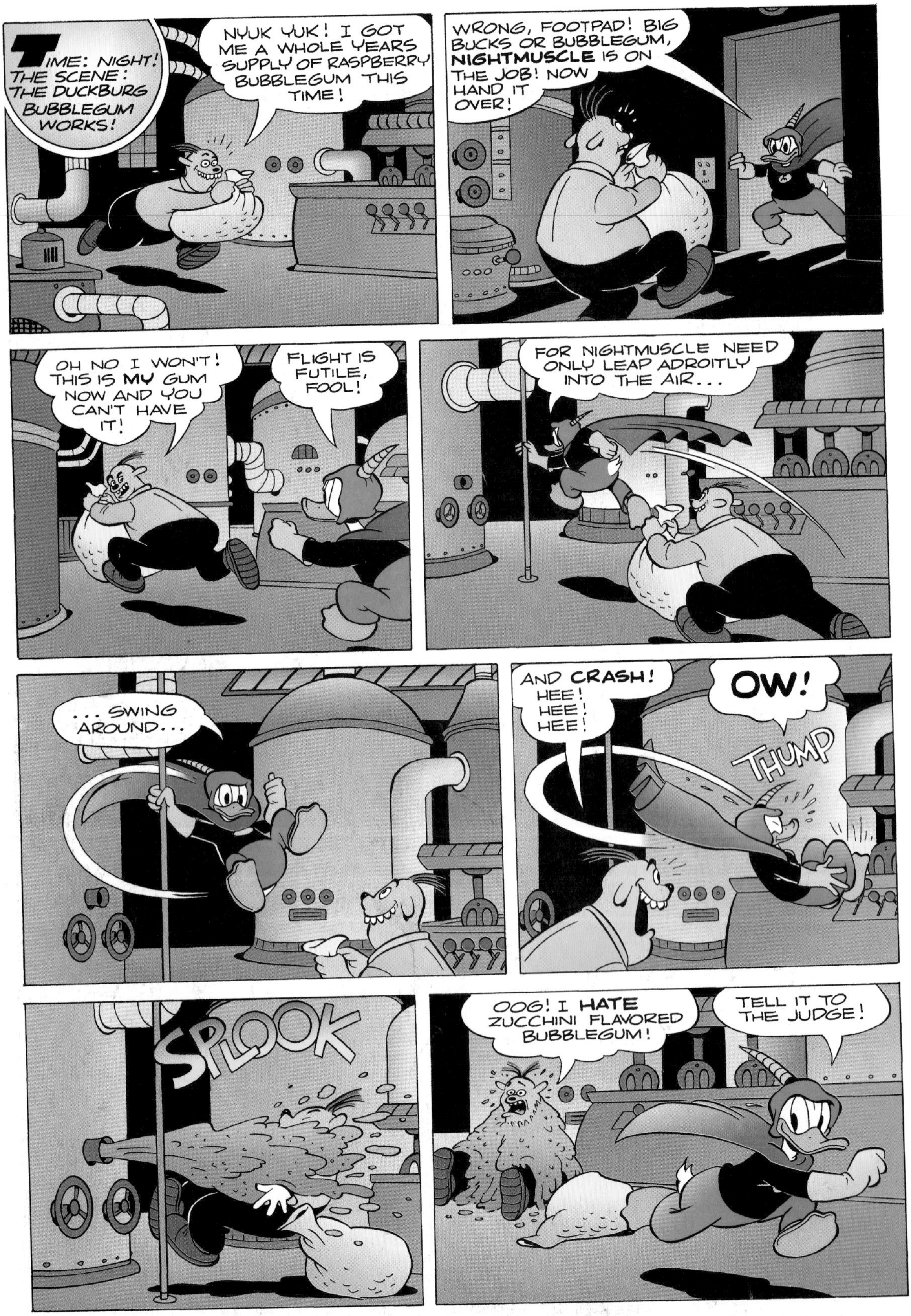
TIME: NIGHT! THE SCENE: THE DUCKBURG BUBBLEGUM WORKS!
NYUK YUK! I GOT ME A WHOLE YEARS SUPPLY OF RASPBERRY BUBBLEGUM THIS TIME!
WRONG, FOOTPAD! BIG BUCKS OR BUBBLEGUM, NIGHTMUSCLE IS ON THE JOB! NOW HAND IT OVER!
OH NO I WON'T! THIS IS MY GUM NOW AND YOU CAN'T HAVE IT!
FLIGHT IS FUTILE, FOOL!
FOR NIGHTMUSCLE NEED ONLY LEAP ADROITLY INTO THE AIR...
... SWING AROUND...
AND CRASH! HEE! HEE! HEE!
OW!
THUMP
SPLOOK
OOG! I HATE ZUCCHINI FLAVORED BUBBLEGUM!
TELL IT TO THE JUDGE!

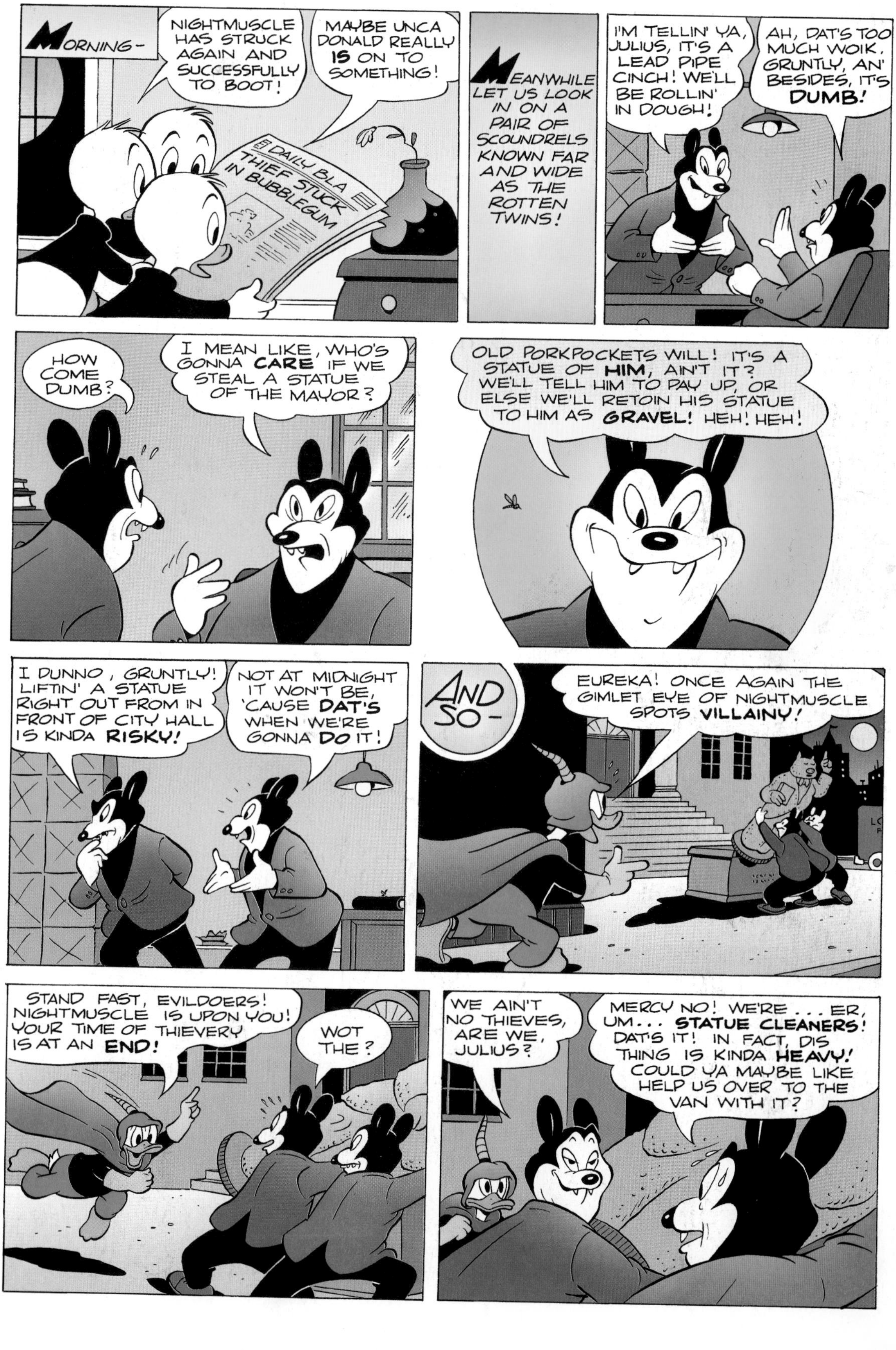
MORNING -
NIGHTMUSCLE HAS STRUCK AGAIN AND SUCCESSFULLY TO BOOT!
MAYBE UNCA DONALD REALLY IS ON TO SOMETHING!
DAILY BLA
THIEF STUCK IN BUBBLEGUM
MEANWHILE LET US LOOK IN ON A PAIR OF SCOUNDRELS KNOWN FAR AND WIDE AS THE ROTTEN TWINS!
I'M TELLIN' YA, JULIUS, IT'S A LEAD PIPE CINCH! WE'LL BE ROLLIN' IN DOUGH!
AH, DAT'S TOO MUCH WOIK, GRUNTLY, AN' BESIDES, IT'S DUMB!
HOW COME DUMB?
I MEAN LIKE, WHO'S GONNA CARE IF WE STEAL A STATUE OF THE MAYOR?
OLD PORKPOCKETS WILL! IT'S A STATUE OF HIM, AIN'T IT? WE'LL TELL HIM TO PAY UP, OR ELSE WE'LL RETOIN HIS STATUE TO HIM AS GRAVEL! HEH! HEH!
I DUNNO, GRUNTLY! LIFTIN' A STATUE RIGHT OUT FROM IN FRONT OF CITY HALL IS KINDA RISKY!
NOT AT MIDNIGHT IT WON'T BE, 'CAUSE DAT'S WHEN WE'RE GONNA DO IT!
AND SO -
EUREKA! ONCE AGAIN THE GIMLET EYE OF NIGHTMUSCLE SPOTS VILLAINY!
STAND FAST, EVILDOERS! NIGHTMUSCLE IS UPON YOU! YOUR TIME OF THIEVERY IS AT AN END!
WOT THE?
WE AIN'T NO THIEVES, ARE WE, JULIUS?
MERCY NO! WE'RE . . . ER, UM . . . STATUE CLEANERS! DAT'S IT! IN FACT, DIS THING IS KINDA HEAVY! COULD YA MAYBE LIKE HELP US OVER TO THE VAN WITH IT?

WELL, I SUPPOSE..

THE MAYOR WILL BE EVER SO **GRATEFUL**, RIGHT, JULIUS?

RIGHT AS RAIN, GRUNTLY!

LOOP'S FRUIT

GRATEFUL? WELL, NOT ACCORDING TO THE MORNING PAPER!

YE CATS! GULP! THIS IS BEYOND AWFUL!

RELAX, UNCA DONALD! YOU CAN'T CATCH THEM **ALL**!

DAILY BLA
STATUE OF MAYOR STOLEN!

OH, I **COULD** HAVE CAUGHT THOSE TWO! TROUBLE IS, THEY FOXED ME AND I **HELPED** THEM!

SIGH! I GUESS WE ALL KNOW WHAT THIS MEANS!

DARN TOOTIN'! TONIGHT NIGHTMUSCLE IS OFF ON A MISSION OF VENGEANCE! NO TWO-BIT CROOKS ARE GOING TO SNOOKER **ME** AND GET AWAY WITH IT!

AND SURE ENOUGH—

NOW, IF I REMEMBER CORRECTLY, THEIR VAN HAD "LOOP'S FRUIT" LETTERED ON IT!

WHICH, TO THE STEEL TRAP MIND OF NIGHTMUSCLE SAYS: **PRODUCE DISTRICT!**

RANGES

ANGES

HMM! SO FAR NOTHING! I WONDER IF THIS IS GOING TO TURN INTO A WILD GOOSE CHASE?

NO, **WAIT!** NIGHTMUSCLE IS **RIGHT!** THAT IS, IF HE SEES WHAT I THINK I SEE!

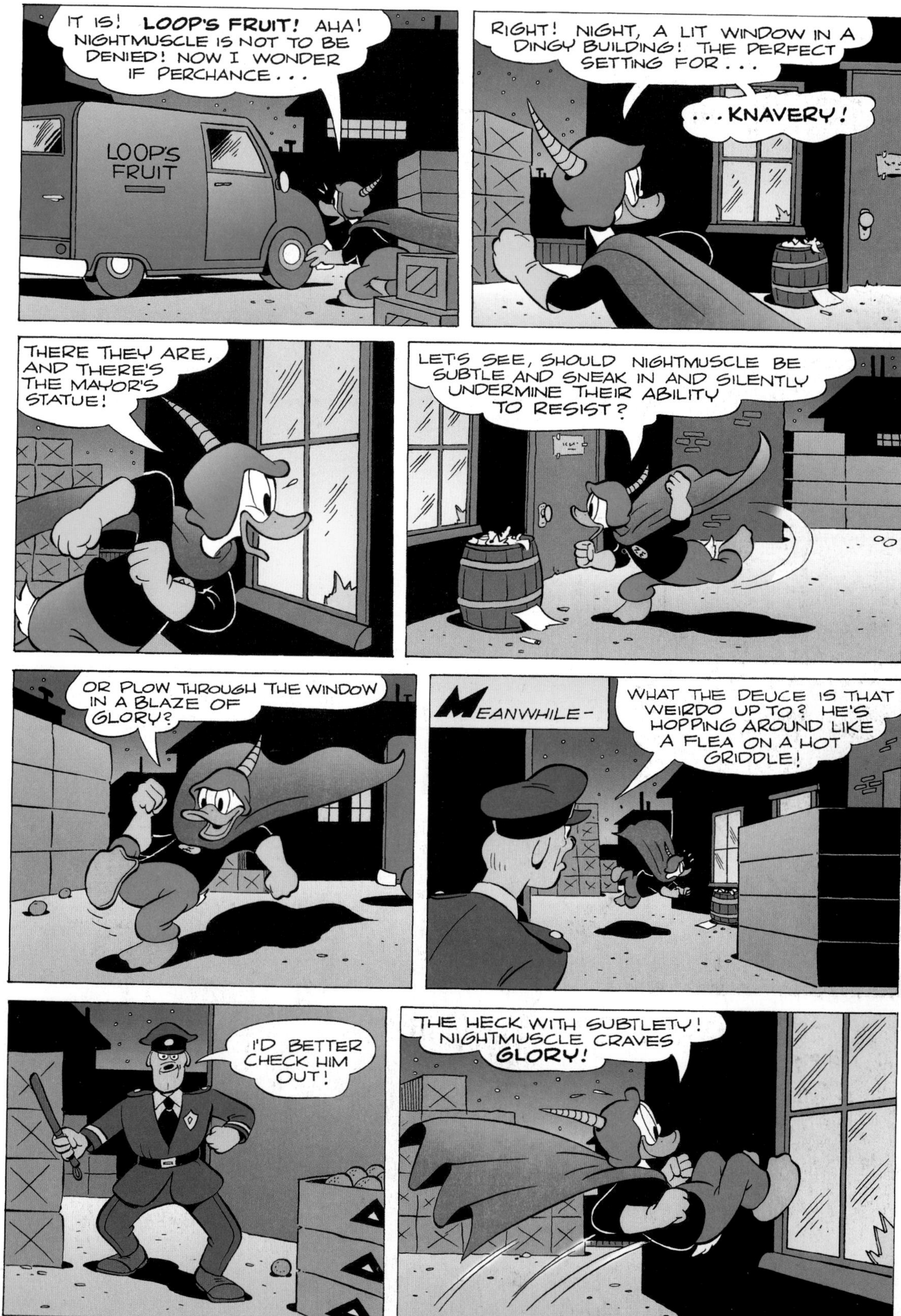
IT IS! LOOP'S FRUIT! AHA! NIGHTMUSCLE IS NOT TO BE DENIED! NOW I WONDER IF PERCHANCE . . .
LOOP'S FRUIT
RIGHT! NIGHT, A LIT WINDOW IN A DINGY BUILDING! THE PERFECT SETTING FOR . . .
. . . KNAVERY!
THERE THEY ARE, AND THERE'S THE MAYOR'S STATUE!
LET'S SEE, SHOULD NIGHTMUSCLE BE SUBTLE AND SNEAK IN AND SILENTLY UNDERMINE THEIR ABILITY TO RESIST?
OR PLOW THROUGH THE WINDOW IN A BLAZE OF GLORY?
MEANWHILE-
WHAT THE DEUCE IS THAT WEIRDO UP TO? HE'S HOPPING AROUND LIKE A FLEA ON A HOT GRIDDLE!
I'D BETTER CHECK HIM OUT!
THE HECK WITH SUBTLETY! NIGHTMUSCLE CRAVES GLORY!

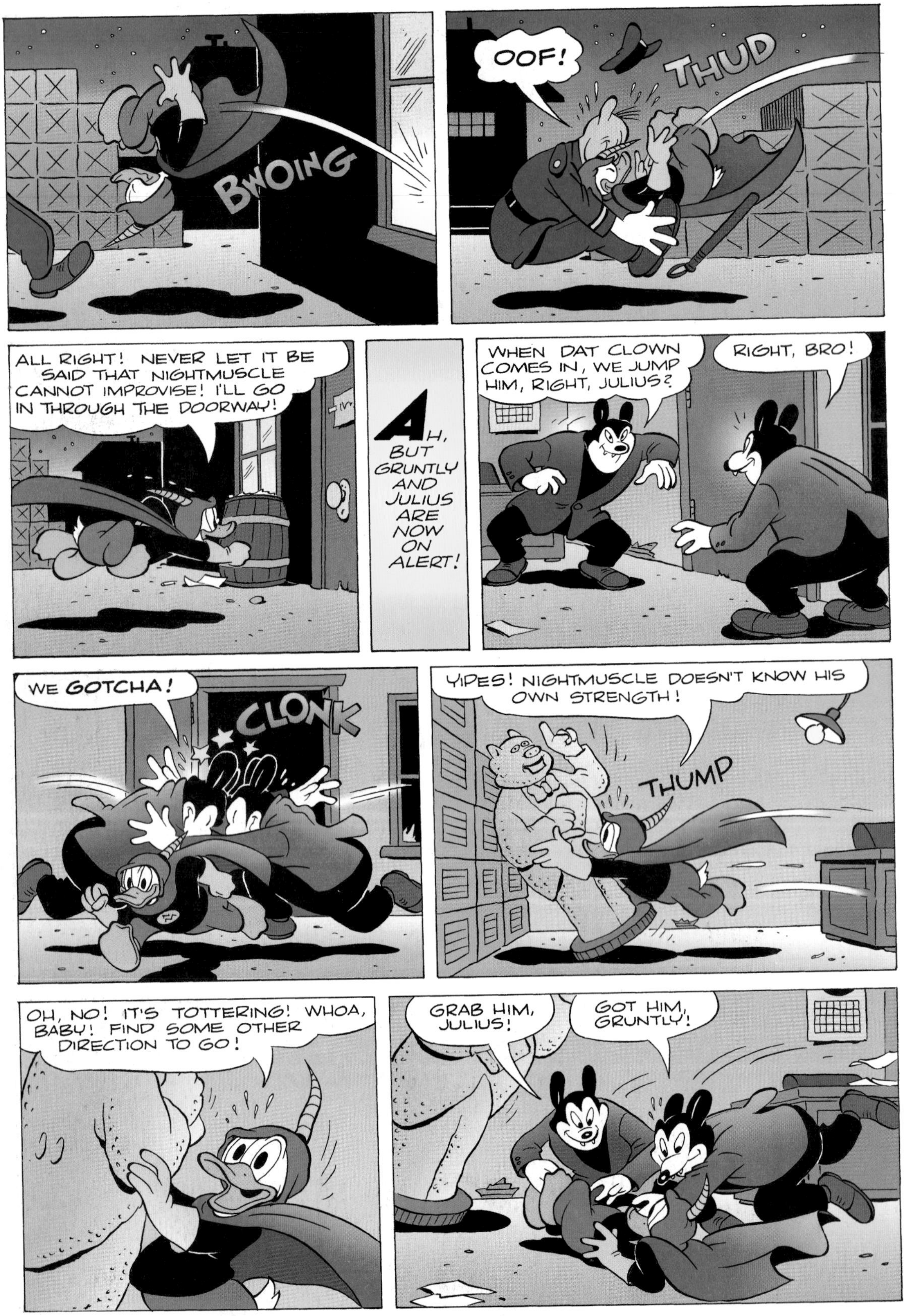
BWOING
OOF!
THUD
ALL RIGHT! NEVER LET IT BE SAID THAT NIGHTMUSCLE CANNOT IMPROVISE! I'LL GO IN THROUGH THE DOORWAY!
AH, BUT GRUNTLY AND JULIUS ARE NOW ON ALERT!
WHEN DAT CLOWN COMES IN, WE JUMP HIM, RIGHT, JULIUS?
RIGHT, BRO!
WE GOTCHA!
CLONK
YIPES! NIGHTMUSCLE DOESN'T KNOW HIS OWN STRENGTH!
THUMP
OH, NO! IT'S TOTTERING! WHOA, BABY! FIND SOME OTHER DIRECTION TO GO!
GRAB HIM, JULIUS!
GOT HIM, GRUNTLY!

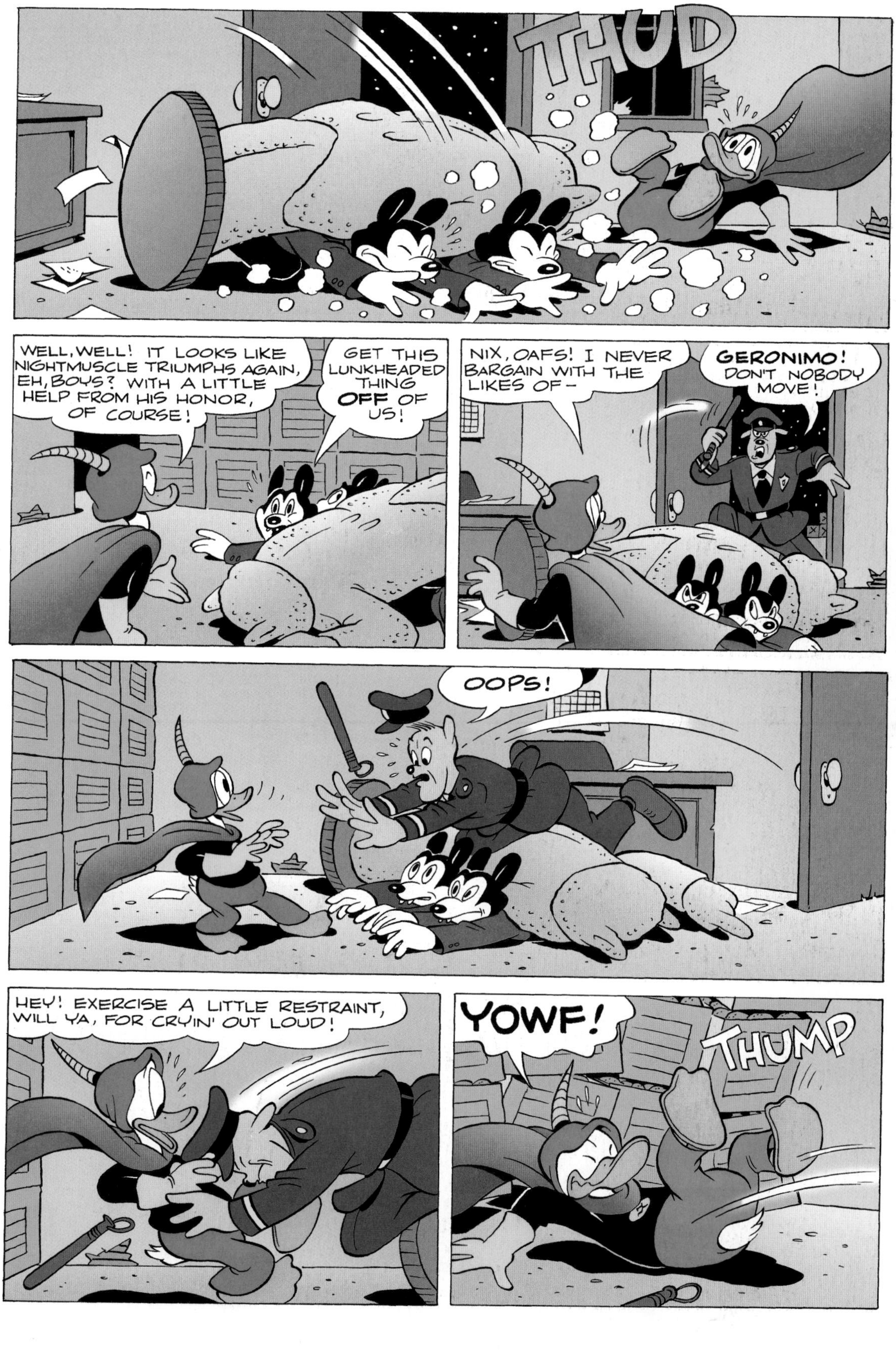
THUD
WELL, WELL! IT LOOKS LIKE NIGHTMUSCLE TRIUMPHS AGAIN, EH, BOYS? WITH A LITTLE HELP FROM HIS HONOR, OF COURSE!
GET THIS LUNKHEADED THING OFF OF US!
NIX, OAFS! I NEVER BARGAIN WITH THE LIKES OF –
GERONIMO! DON'T NOBODY MOVE!
OOPS!
HEY! EXERCISE A LITTLE RESTRAINT, WILL YA, FOR CRYIN' OUT LOUD!
YOWF!
THUMP

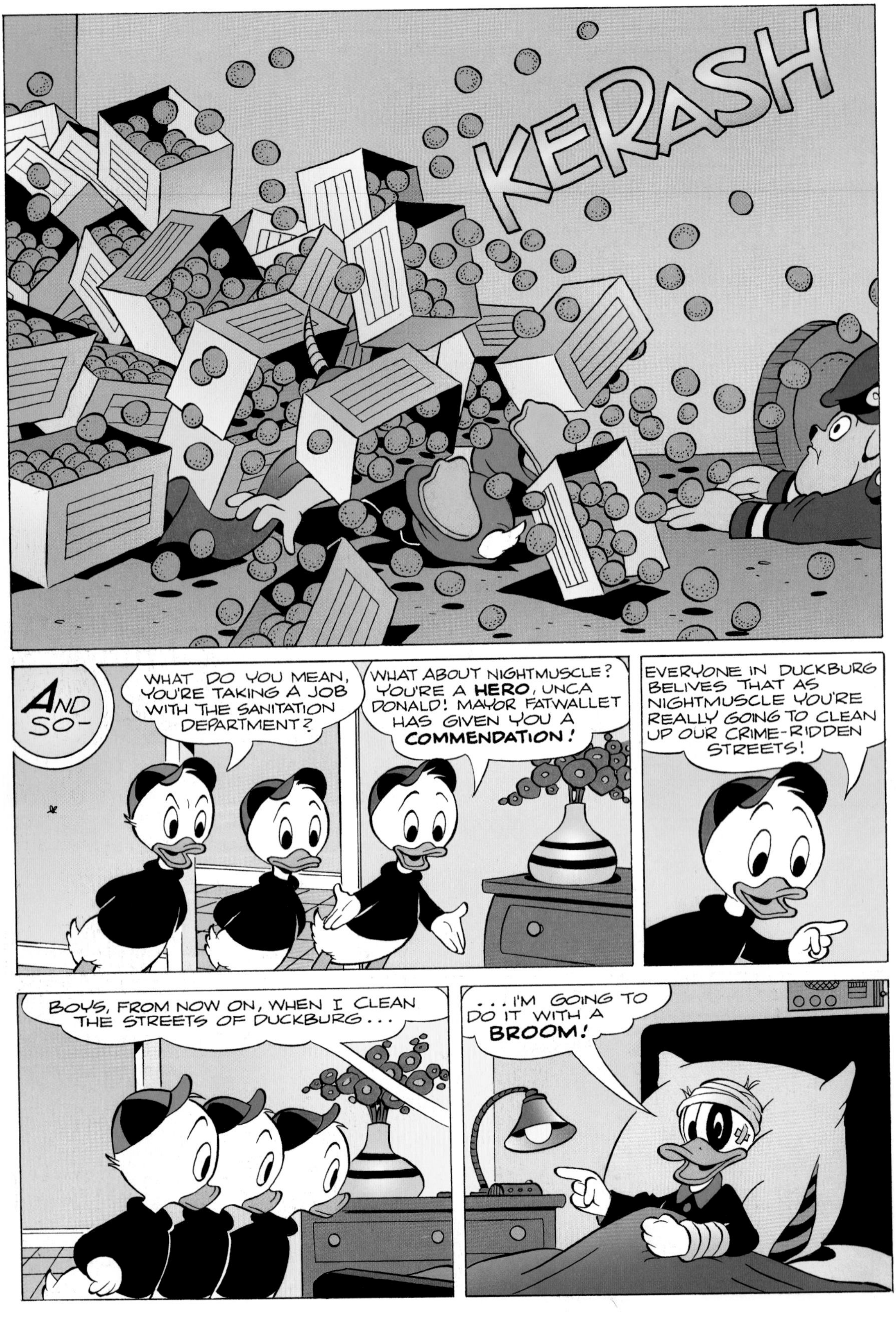
KERASH
AND SO-
WHAT DO YOU MEAN, YOU'RE TAKING A JOB WITH THE SANITATION DEPARTMENT?
WHAT ABOUT NIGHTMUSCLE? YOU'RE A **HERO**, UNCA DONALD! MAYOR FATWALLET HAS GIVEN YOU A **COMMENDATION**!
EVERYONE IN DUCKBURG BELIVES THAT AS NIGHTMUSCLE YOU'RE REALLY GOING TO CLEAN UP OUR CRIME-RIDDEN STREETS!
BOYS, FROM NOW ON, WHEN I CLEAN THE STREETS OF DUCKBURG...
...I'M GOING TO DO IT WITH A **BROOM**!

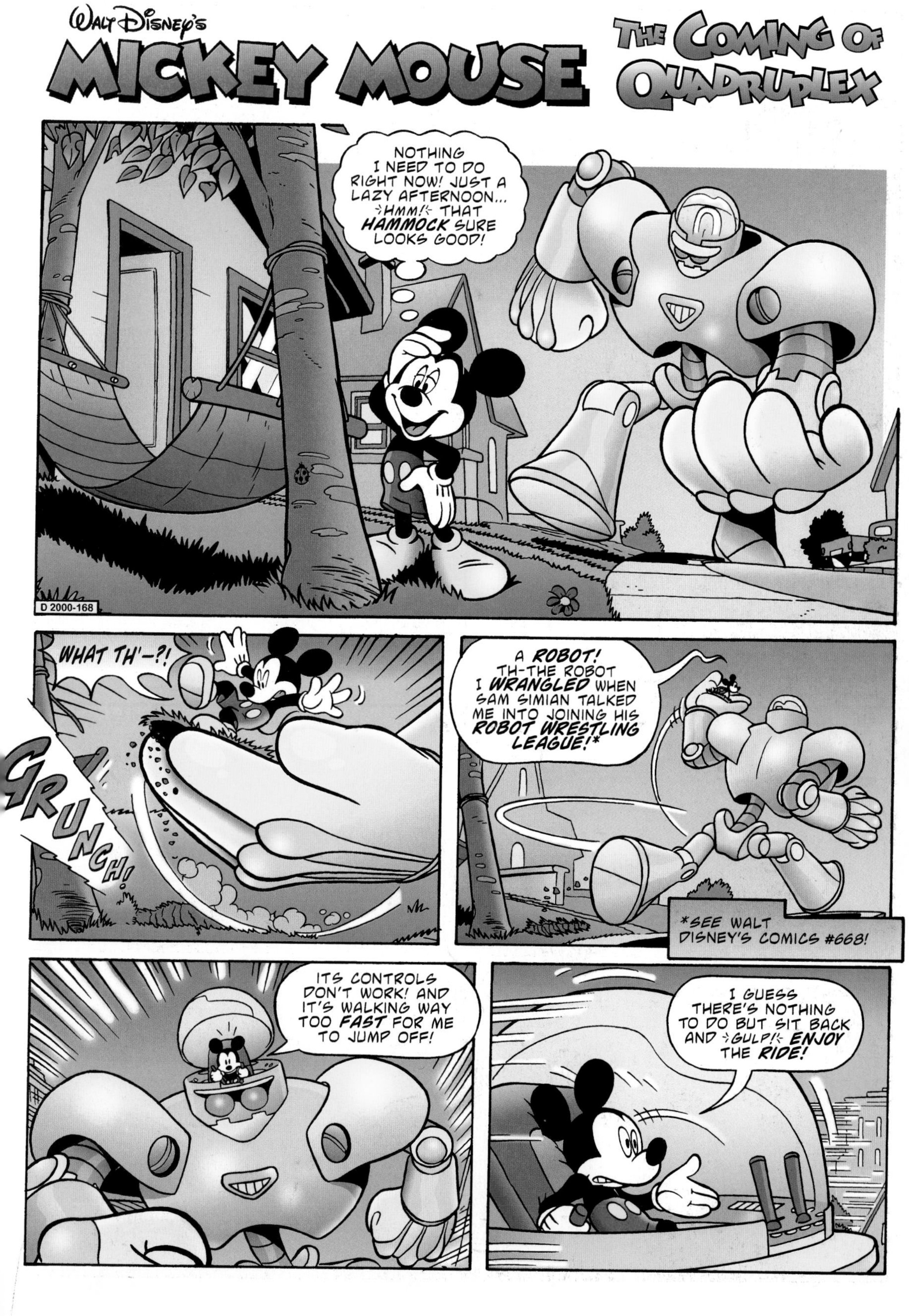
Walt Disney's MICKEY MOUSE
THE COMING OF QUADRUPLEX
NOTHING I NEED TO DO RIGHT NOW! JUST A LAZY AFTERNOON... *HMM!* THAT HAMMOCK SURE LOOKS GOOD!
D 2000-168
WHAT TH'-?!
GRUNCH!
A ROBOT! TH-THE ROBOT I WRANGLED WHEN SAM SIMIAN TALKED ME INTO JOINING HIS ROBOT WRESTLING LEAGUE!*
*SEE WALT DISNEY'S COMICS #668!
ITS CONTROLS DON'T WORK! AND IT'S WALKING WAY TOO FAST FOR ME TO JUMP OFF!
I GUESS THERE'S NOTHING TO DO BUT SIT BACK AND *GULP!* ENJOY THE RIDE!

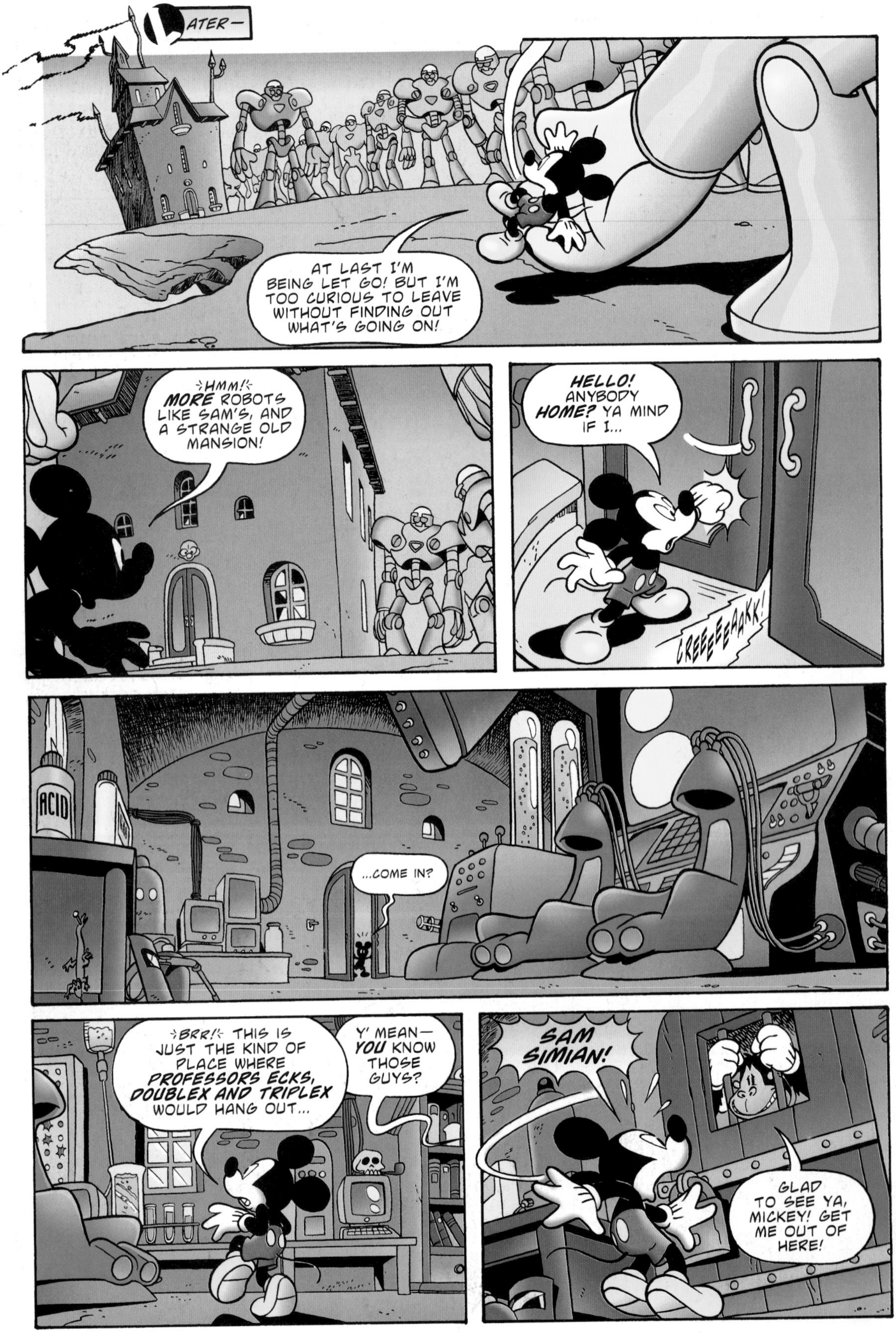
LATER—
AT LAST I'M BEING LET GO! BUT I'M TOO CURIOUS TO LEAVE WITHOUT FINDING OUT WHAT'S GOING ON!
HMM! MORE ROBOTS LIKE SAM'S, AND A STRANGE OLD MANSION!
HELLO! ANYBODY HOME? YA MIND IF I...
CREEEEEAAKK!
ACID
...COME IN?
BRR! THIS IS JUST THE KIND OF PLACE WHERE PROFESSORS ECKS, DOUBLEX AND TRIPLEX WOULD HANG OUT...
Y' MEAN— YOU KNOW THOSE GUYS?
SAM SIMIAN!
GLAD TO SEE YA, MICKEY! GET ME OUT OF HERE!

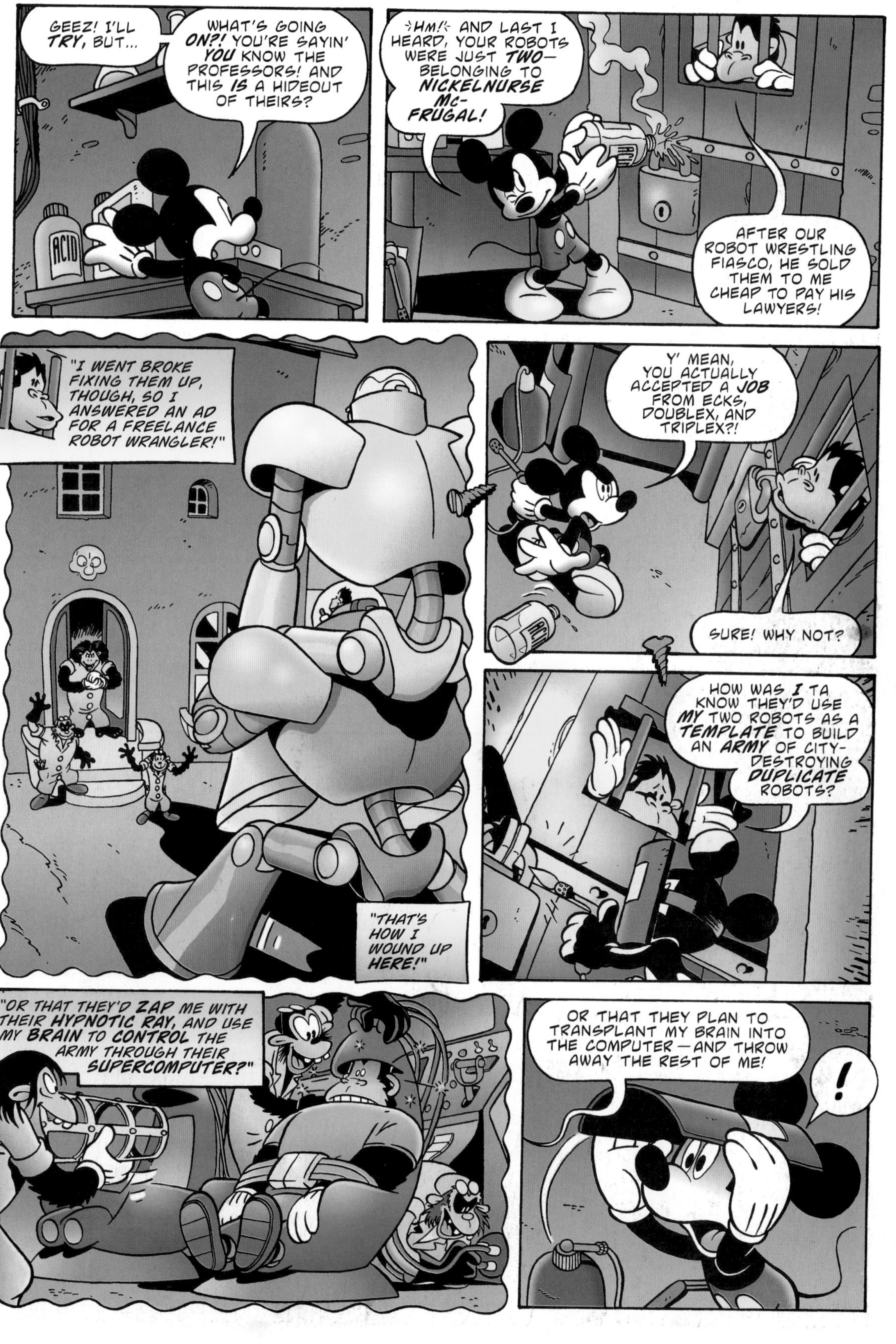
GEEZ! I'LL TRY, BUT...
WHAT'S GOING ON?! YOU'RE SAYIN' YOU KNOW THE PROFESSORS! AND THIS IS A HIDEOUT OF THEIRS?
HM! AND LAST I HEARD, YOUR ROBOTS WERE JUST TWO— BELONGING TO NICKELNURSE Mc-FRUGAL!
AFTER OUR ROBOT WRESTLING FIASCO, HE SOLD THEM TO ME CHEAP TO PAY HIS LAWYERS!
"I WENT BROKE FIXING THEM UP, THOUGH, SO I ANSWERED AN AD FOR A FREELANCE ROBOT WRANGLER!"
"THAT'S HOW I WOUND UP HERE!"
Y' MEAN, YOU ACTUALLY ACCEPTED A JOB FROM ECKS, DOUBLEX, AND TRIPLEX?!
SURE! WHY NOT?
HOW WAS I TA KNOW THEY'D USE MY TWO ROBOTS AS A TEMPLATE TO BUILD AN ARMY OF CITY-DESTROYING DUPLICATE ROBOTS?
"OR THAT THEY'D ZAP ME WITH THEIR HYPNOTIC RAY, AND USE MY BRAIN TO CONTROL THE ARMY THROUGH THEIR SUPERCOMPUTER?"
OR THAT THEY PLAN TO TRANSPLANT MY BRAIN INTO THE COMPUTER—AND THROW AWAY THE REST OF ME!
!

F' GOSH *SAKES*, SAM!

YEAH, IT'S *BAD!* THEY'RE OUT BUYING SUPPLIES FOR THE OPERATION RIGHT NOW!

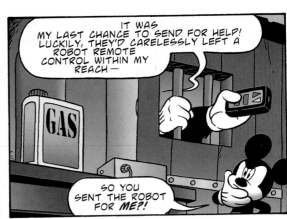

IT WAS MY LAST CHANCE TO SEND FOR HELP! LUCKILY, THEY'D CARELESSLY LEFT A ROBOT REMOTE CONTROL WITHIN MY REACH—

SO YOU SENT THE ROBOT FOR *ME?!*

WHY NOT GET THE *COPS?* OR MAKE THE ROBOT BASH IN HERE IT-SELF AND RESCUE YOU!

I... I...

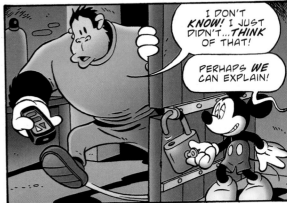

I DON'T *KNOW!* I JUST DIDN'T...*THINK* OF THAT!

PERHAPS *WE* CAN EXPLAIN!

THE PROFES-SORS!

SAM ONLY *THOUGHT* HE SENT FOR *HELP!* ⸓HEE! HEE!⸕ ACTUALLY, HE WAS UNDER *POST-HYPNOTIC SUGGESTION* TO BRING US A *SECOND ROBOT WRANGLER!*

OUR SUPERCOMPUTER, *QUADRUPLEX*, WILL BE SMART WITH *ONE* TRANSPLANTED HUMAN BRAIN! BUT WITH *TWO* BRAINS, HE'LL BE EVEN *SMARTER!*

WHAT A PLEASANT SURPRISE THAT HIS *SECOND* BRAIN SHOULD BE THAT OF OUR OLD FOE— *MICKEY MOUSE!*

NOT IF WE CAN GET TO OUR ROBOTS AND ESCAPE! RUSH 'EM, MICKEY!
SAM... LOOK OUT!
GASP!
THUNK!
THAT WAY, SAM!
THANKS, MICKEY!
HOW DID YOU KNOW THEY HAD A TRAP-DOOR?
THEIR HIDEOUTS ALWAYS HAVE TRAPDOORS!
CONTROLS STILL DON'T WORK!
THE PROFS MUST BE OVER-RIDING THEM WITH SAM'S RE-MOTE!
YIKES! THE HYPNOTIC RAY!

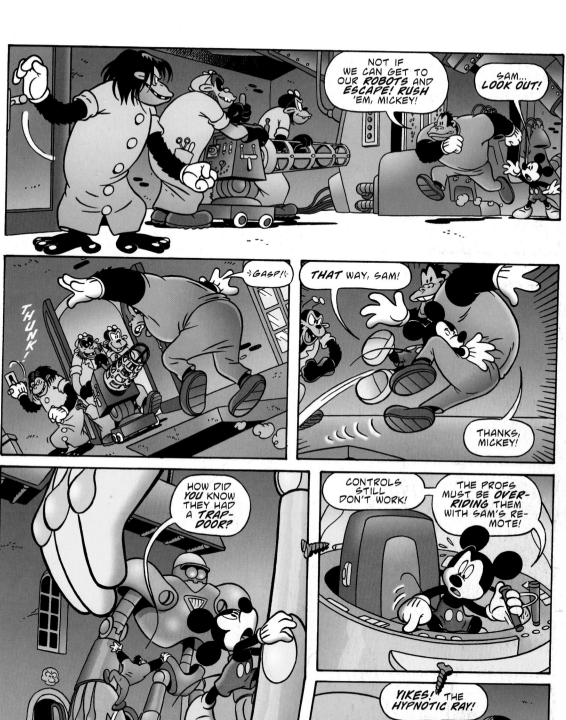

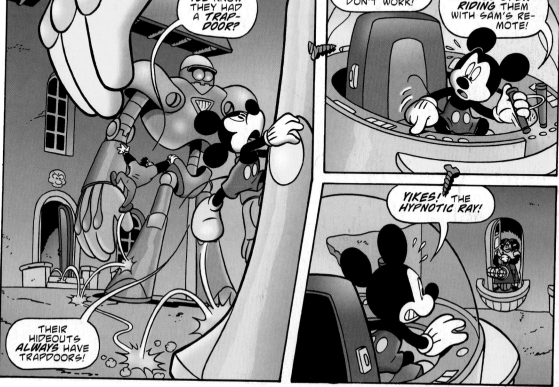

I CAN DODGE THE RAY BY HIDING UNDER HERE! BUT I'M STILL UP A CREEK IF I CAN'T CONTROL THIS ROBOT!
SNAP!
CRACKLE!
THAT BLUE WIRING HARNESS— IT'S NEW! I BET IT ENABLES THE REMOTE!
NOTHING TO LOSE IF I...
SNAP
ALL RIGHT! THE CONTROLS WORK AGAIN!
SAM HERE! MY CONTROLS DON'T WORK...
...AND THE PROFESSORS ARE MAKING ME ATTACK YOU!
THERE'S A BLUE WIRING HARNESS UNDER YOUR DASHBOARD, SAM! YANK IT OUT!
IT WORKED, MICK! THANKS!
HEY!
KRINK!
I CAN'T LAND RIGHT, SAM! I THOUGHT YOU FIXED THE ROBOTS UP!
I NEVER SAID I'D DONE A PERFECT JOB! SEE HOW MY ROBOT LIMPS?
WHAT'S THAT CLANKING NOISE?
CLANK
CLANK

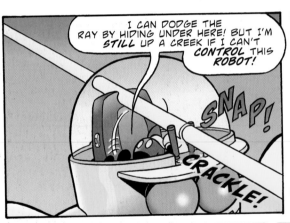

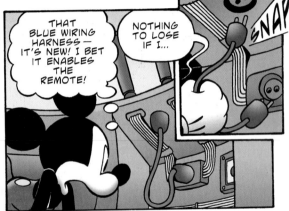

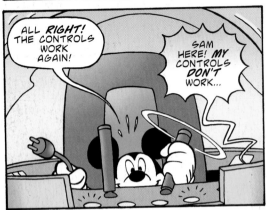

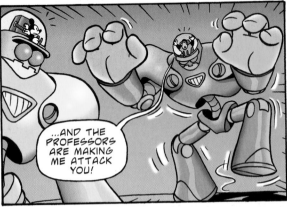

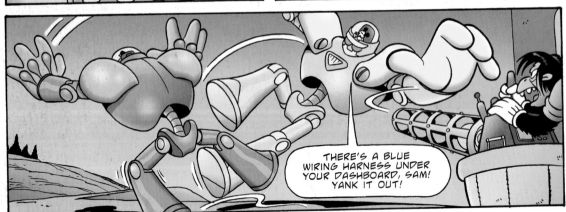

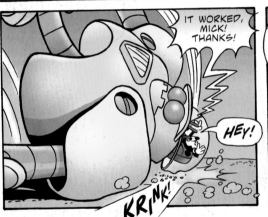

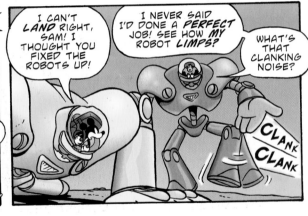

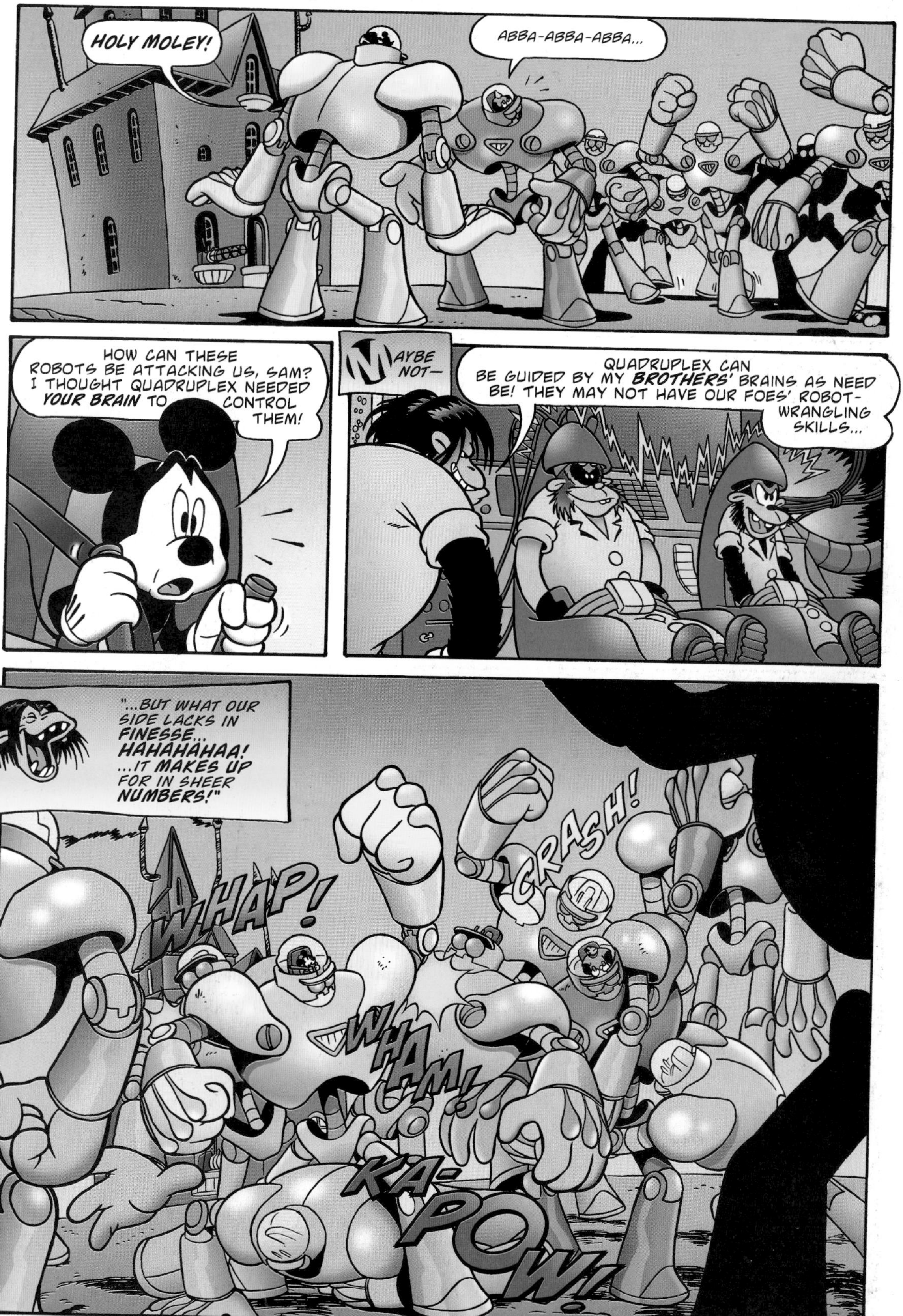
HOLY MOLEY!
ABBA-ABBA-ABBA...
HOW CAN THESE ROBOTS BE ATTACKING US, SAM? I THOUGHT QUADRUPLEX NEEDED YOUR BRAIN TO CONTROL THEM!
MAYBE NOT—
QUADRUPLEX CAN BE GUIDED BY MY BROTHERS' BRAINS AS NEED BE! THEY MAY NOT HAVE OUR FOES' ROBOT-WRANGLING SKILLS...
"...BUT WHAT OUR SIDE LACKS IN FINESSE... HAHAHAHAA! ...IT MAKES UP FOR IN SHEER NUMBERS!"
CRASH!
WHAP!
WHAM!
KA-POW!

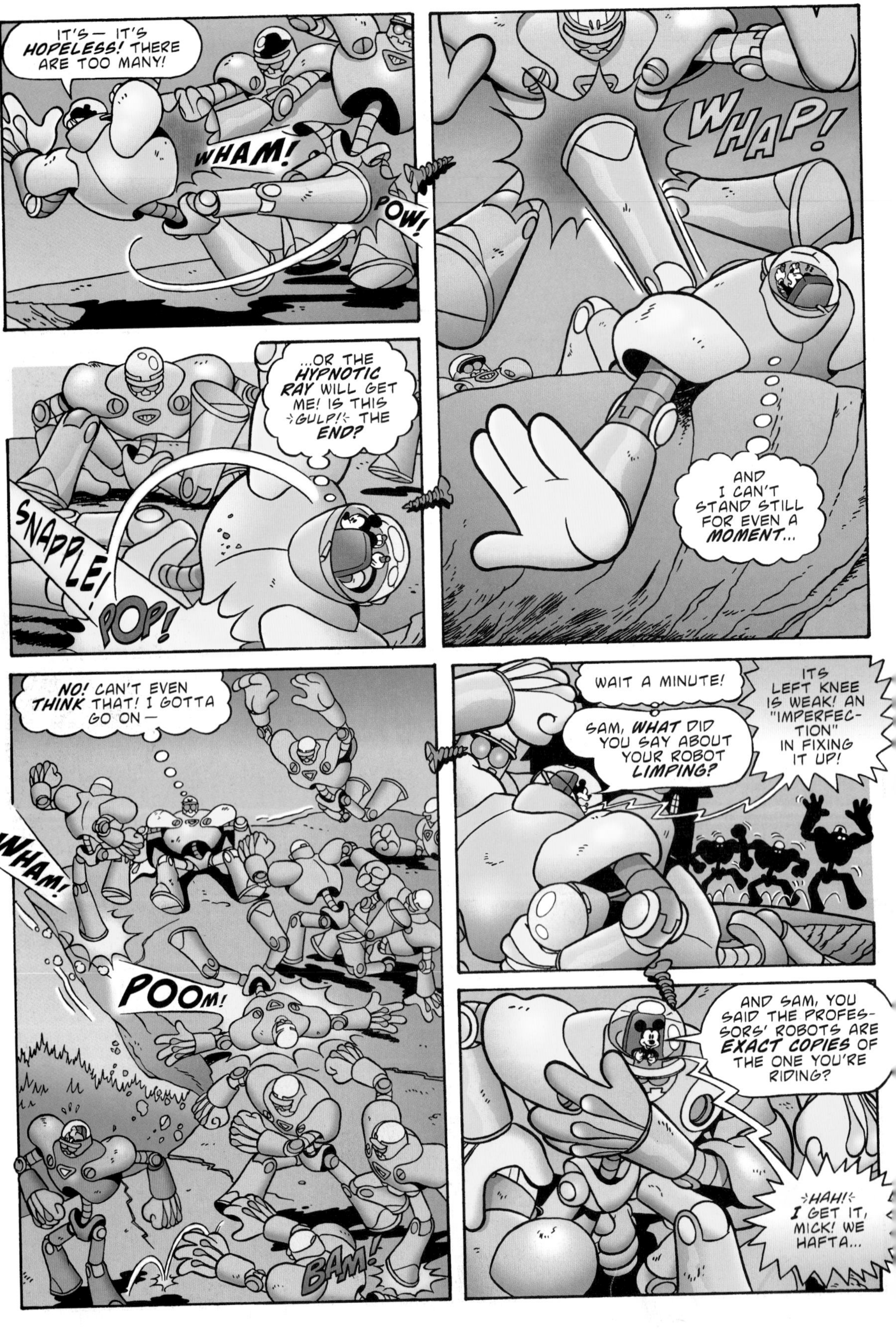
IT'S— IT'S HOPELESS! THERE ARE TOO MANY!
WHAM!
POW!
WHAP!
...OR THE HYPNOTIC RAY WILL GET ME! IS THIS *GULP!* THE END?
SNAPPLE!
POP!
AND I CAN'T STAND STILL FOR EVEN A MOMENT...
NO! CAN'T EVEN THINK THAT! I GOTTA GO ON—
WHAM!
POOM!
BAM!
WAIT A MINUTE!
SAM, WHAT DID YOU SAY ABOUT YOUR ROBOT LIMPING?
ITS LEFT KNEE IS WEAK! AN "IMPERFECTION" IN FIXING IT UP!
AND SAM, YOU SAID THE PROFESSORS' ROBOTS ARE EXACT COPIES OF THE ONE YOU'RE RIDING?
HAH! I GET IT, MICK! WE HAFTA...

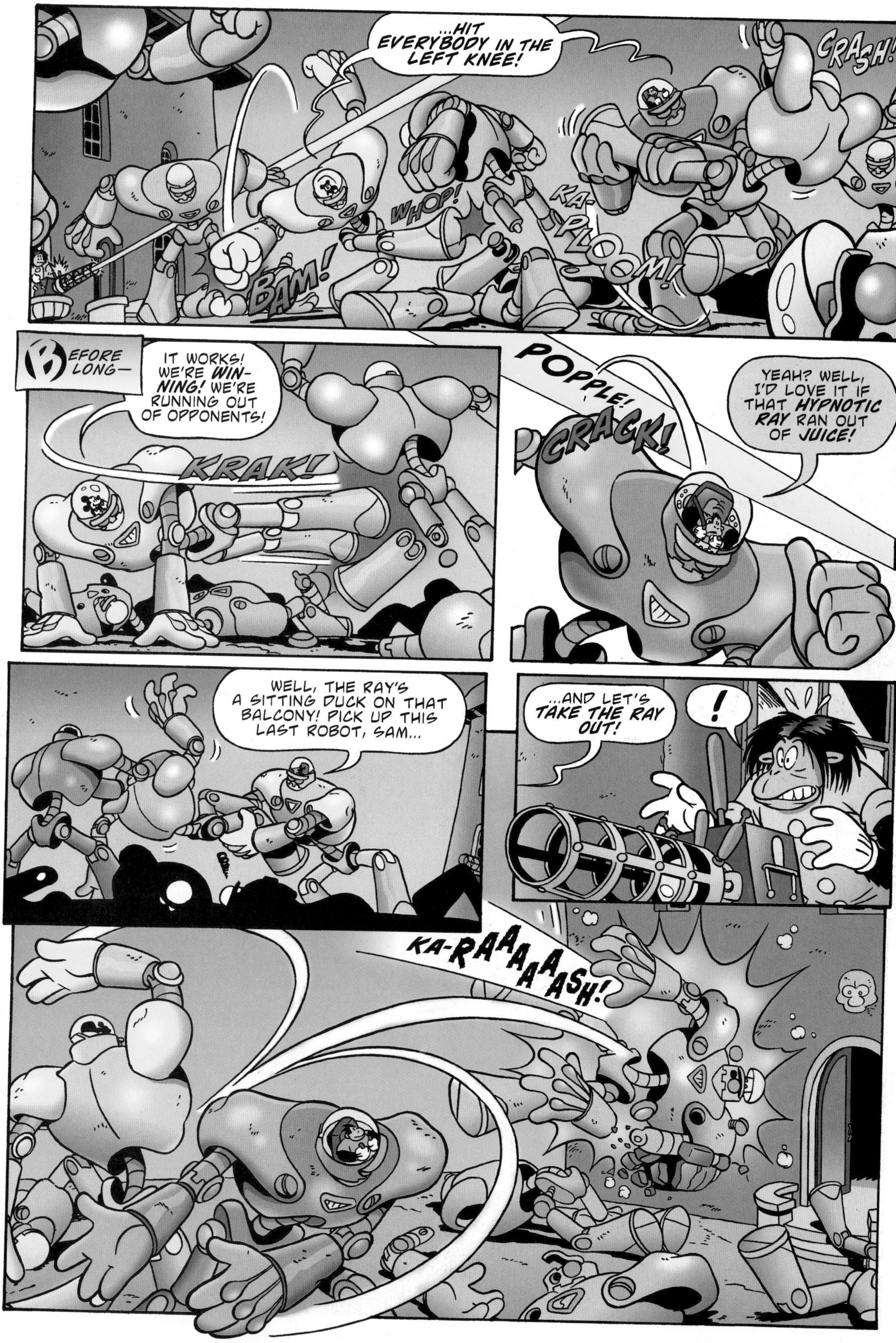
...HIT EVERYBODY IN THE LEFT KNEE!
CRASH!
WHOP!
KA-PLOOM!
BAM!
BEFORE LONG—
IT WORKS! WE'RE WIN-NING! WE'RE RUNNING OUT OF OPPONENTS!
KRAK!
POPPLE!
CRACK!
YEAH? WELL, I'D LOVE IT IF THAT HYPNOTIC RAY RAN OUT OF JUICE!
WELL, THE RAY'S A SITTING DUCK ON THAT BALCONY! PICK UP THIS LAST ROBOT, SAM...
...AND LET'S TAKE THE RAY OUT!
!
KA-RAAAAAASH!

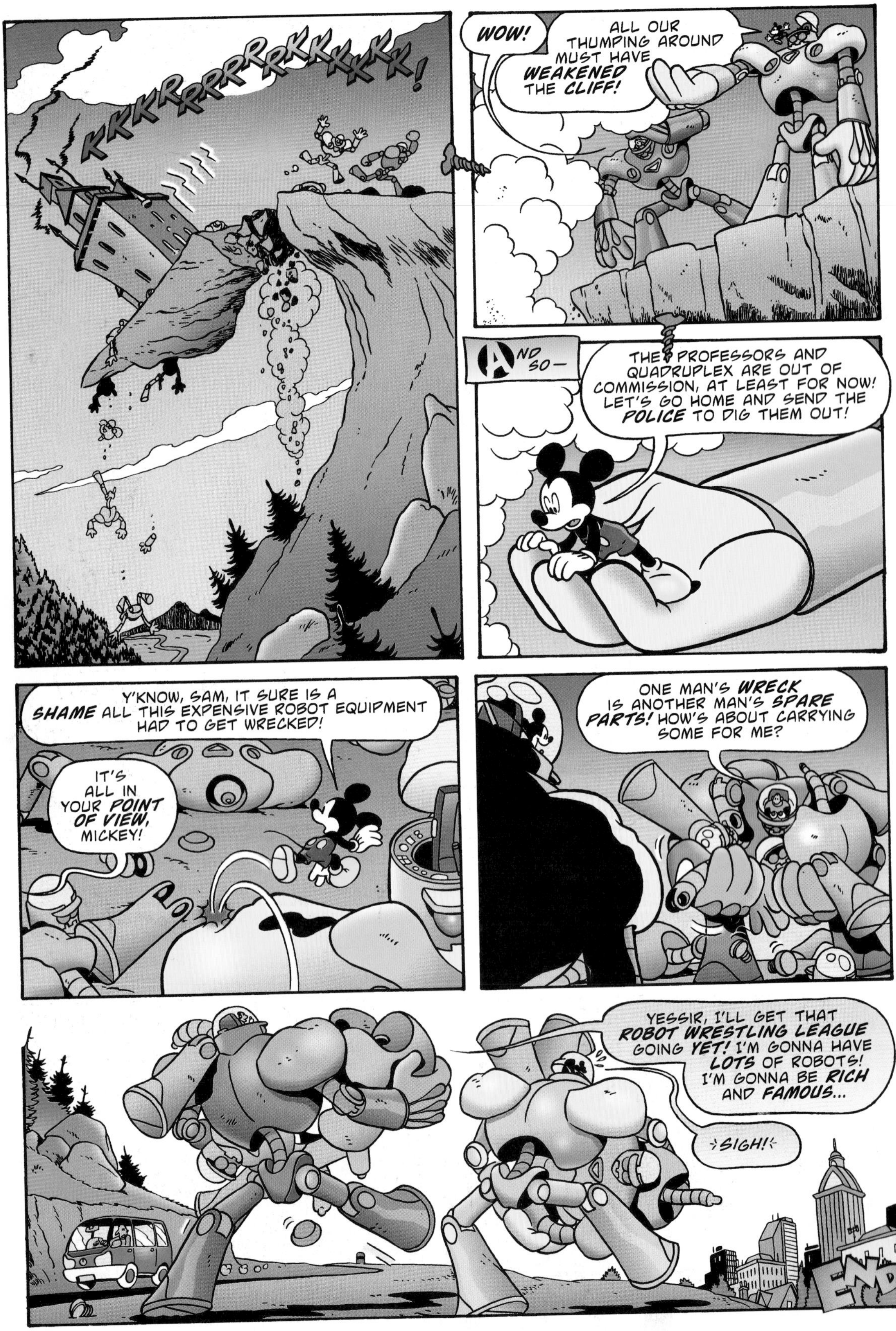
KKKRRRRRRKKKKKK!
WOW!
ALL OUR THUMPING AROUND MUST HAVE WEAKENED THE CLIFF!
AND SO—
THE PROFESSORS AND QUADRUPLEX ARE OUT OF COMMISSION, AT LEAST FOR NOW! LET'S GO HOME AND SEND THE POLICE TO DIG THEM OUT!
Y'KNOW, SAM, IT SURE IS A SHAME ALL THIS EXPENSIVE ROBOT EQUIPMENT HAD TO GET WRECKED!
IT'S ALL IN YOUR POINT OF VIEW, MICKEY!
ONE MAN'S WRECK IS ANOTHER MAN'S SPARE PARTS! HOW'S ABOUT CARRYING SOME FOR ME?
YESSIR, I'LL GET THAT ROBOT WRESTLING LEAGUE GOING YET! I'M GONNA HAVE LOTS OF ROBOTS! I'M GONNA BE RICH AND FAMOUS...
SIGH!
END

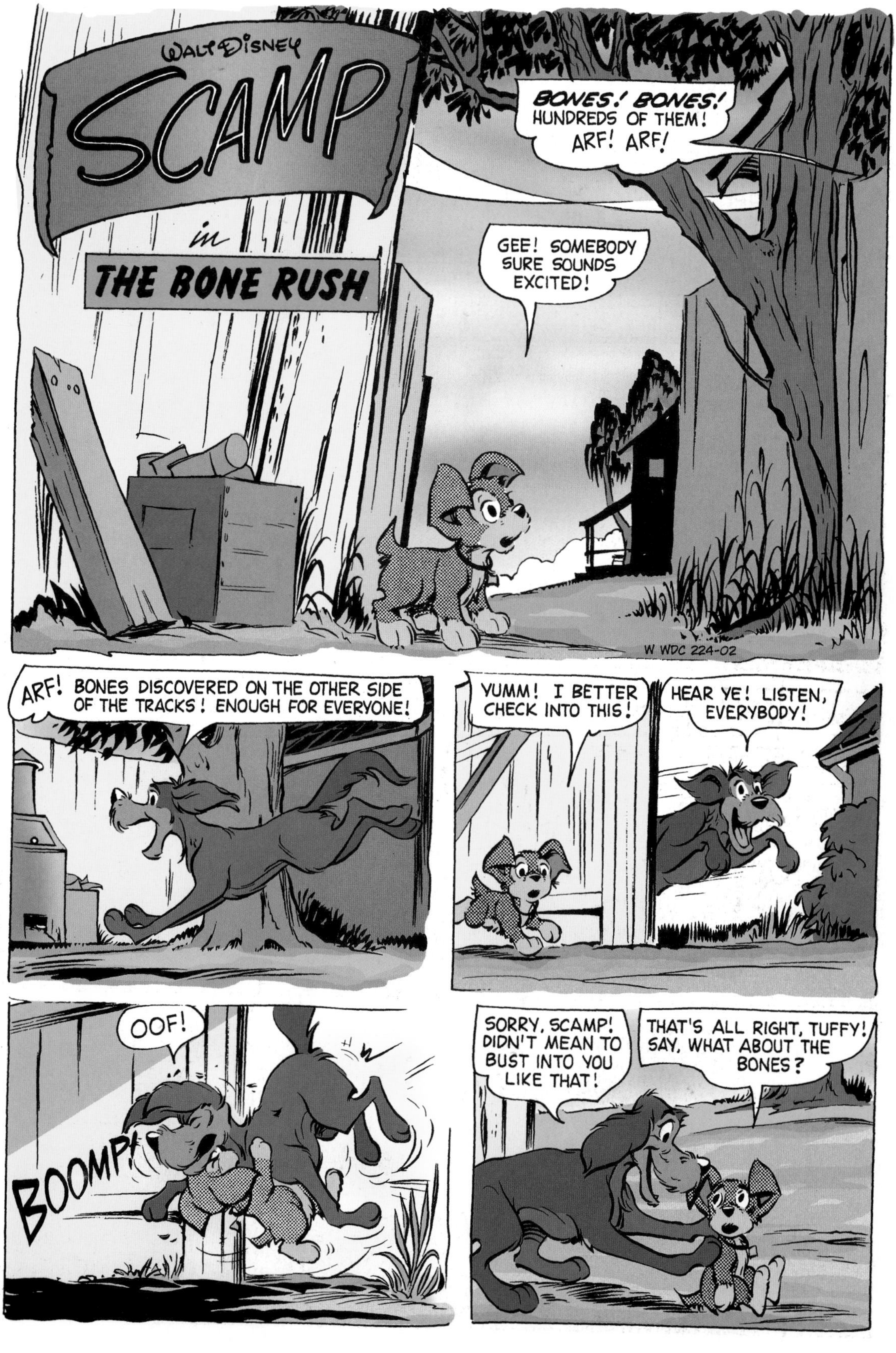
WALT DISNEY
SCAMP
in
THE BONE RUSH
BONES! BONES! HUNDREDS OF THEM! ARF! ARF!
GEE! SOMEBODY SURE SOUNDS EXCITED!
W WDC 224-02
ARF! BONES DISCOVERED ON THE OTHER SIDE OF THE TRACKS! ENOUGH FOR EVERYONE!
YUMM! I BETTER CHECK INTO THIS!
HEAR YE! LISTEN, EVERYBODY!
OOF!
BOOMP!
SORRY, SCAMP! DIDN'T MEAN TO BUST INTO YOU LIKE THAT!
THAT'S ALL RIGHT, TUFFY! SAY, WHAT ABOUT THE BONES?

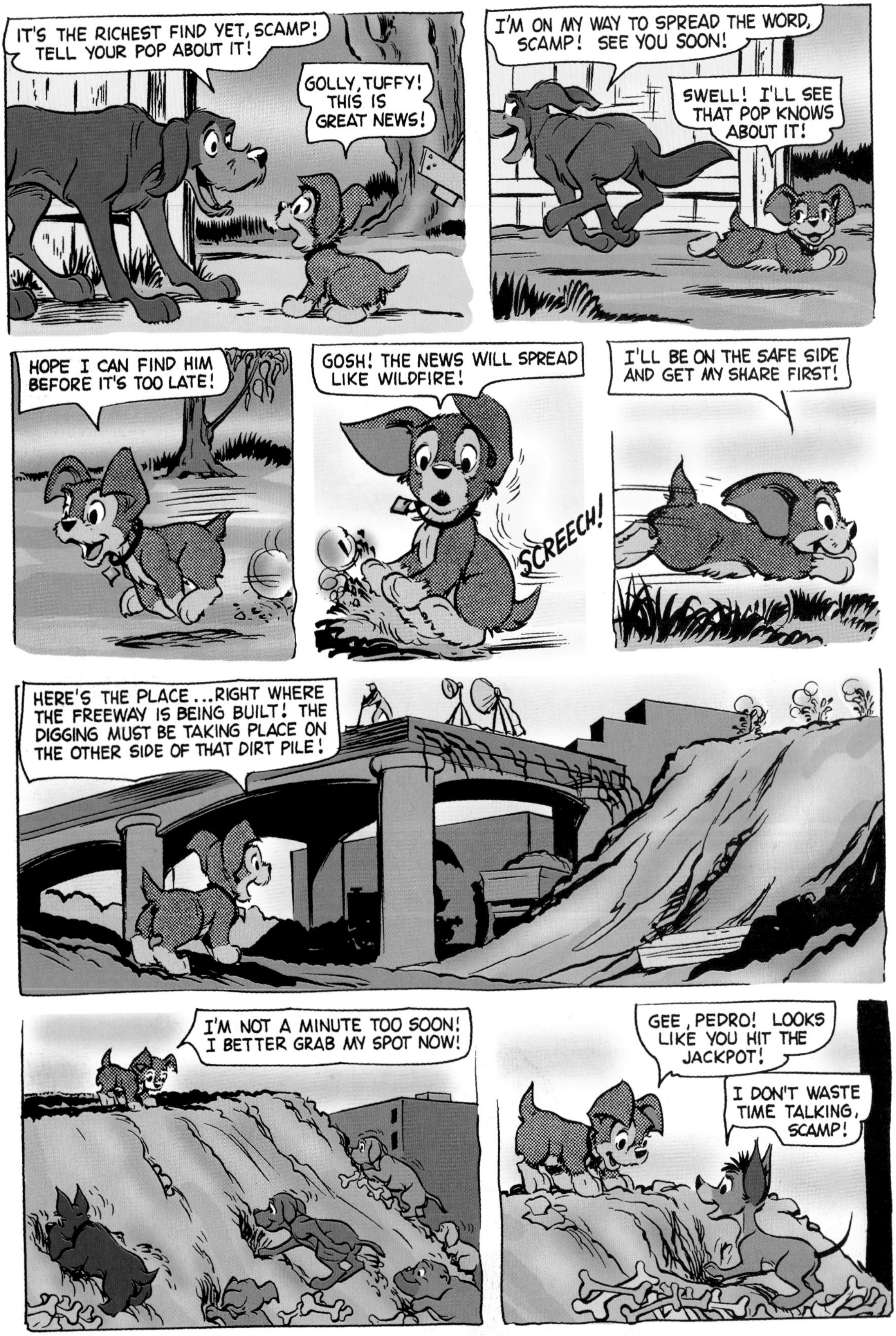
IT'S THE RICHEST FIND YET, SCAMP! TELL YOUR POP ABOUT IT!
GOLLY, TUFFY! THIS IS GREAT NEWS!
I'M ON MY WAY TO SPREAD THE WORD, SCAMP! SEE YOU SOON!
SWELL! I'LL SEE THAT POP KNOWS ABOUT IT!
HOPE I CAN FIND HIM BEFORE IT'S TOO LATE!
GOSH! THE NEWS WILL SPREAD LIKE WILDFIRE!
SCREECH!
I'LL BE ON THE SAFE SIDE AND GET MY SHARE FIRST!
HERE'S THE PLACE...RIGHT WHERE THE FREEWAY IS BEING BUILT! THE DIGGING MUST BE TAKING PLACE ON THE OTHER SIDE OF THAT DIRT PILE!
I'M NOT A MINUTE TOO SOON! I BETTER GRAB MY SPOT NOW!
GEE, PEDRO! LOOKS LIKE YOU HIT THE JACKPOT!
I DON'T WASTE TIME TALKING, SCAMP!

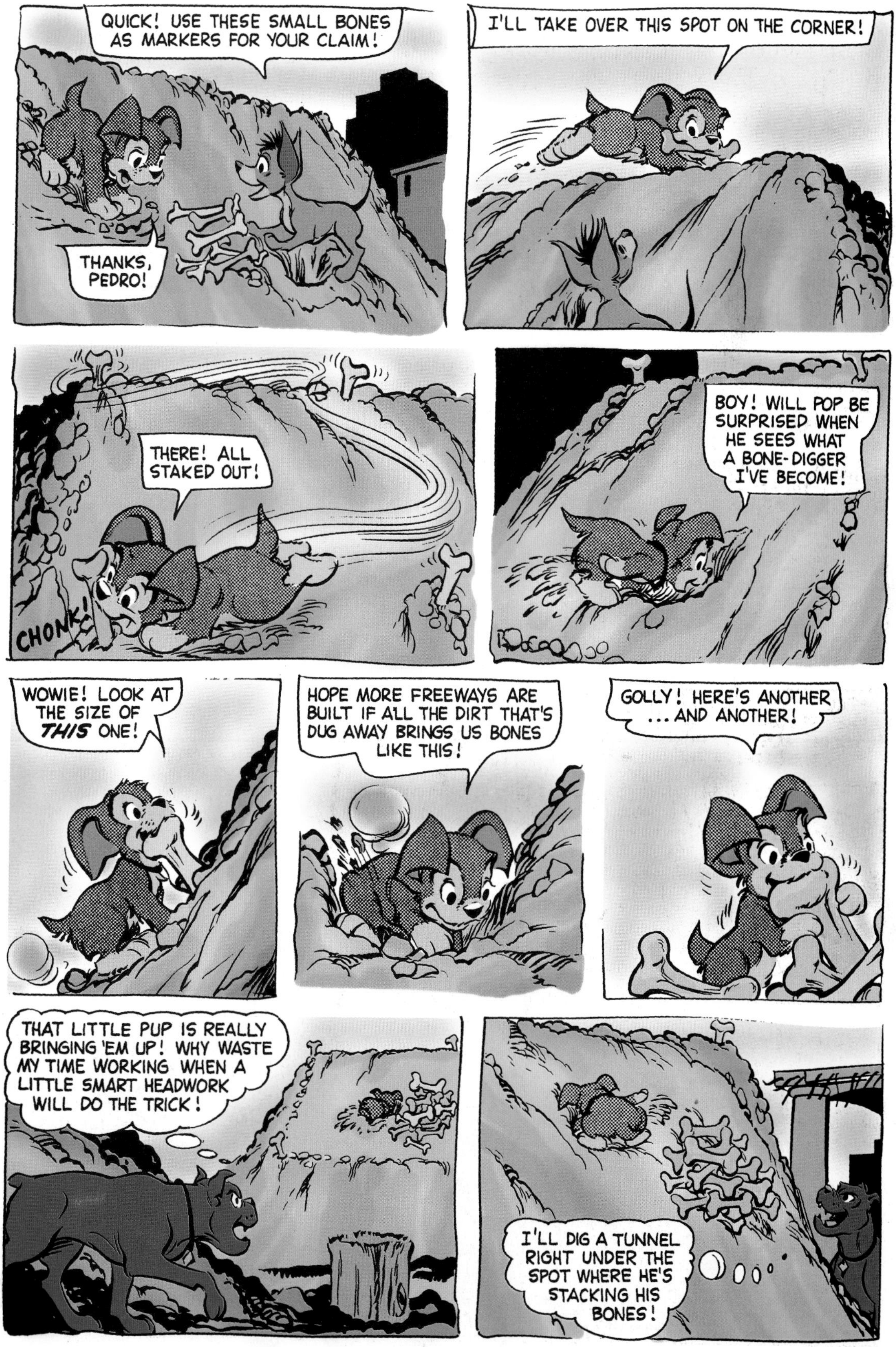
QUICK! USE THESE SMALL BONES AS MARKERS FOR YOUR CLAIM!
THANKS, PEDRO!
I'LL TAKE OVER THIS SPOT ON THE CORNER!
THERE! ALL STAKED OUT!
CHONK!
BOY! WILL POP BE SURPRISED WHEN HE SEES WHAT A BONE-DIGGER I'VE BECOME!
WOWIE! LOOK AT THE SIZE OF THIS ONE!
HOPE MORE FREEWAYS ARE BUILT IF ALL THE DIRT THAT'S DUG AWAY BRINGS US BONES LIKE THIS!
GOLLY! HERE'S ANOTHER ... AND ANOTHER!
THAT LITTLE PUP IS REALLY BRINGING 'EM UP! WHY WASTE MY TIME WORKING WHEN A LITTLE SMART HEADWORK WILL DO THE TRICK!
I'LL DIG A TUNNEL RIGHT UNDER THE SPOT WHERE HE'S STACKING HIS BONES!

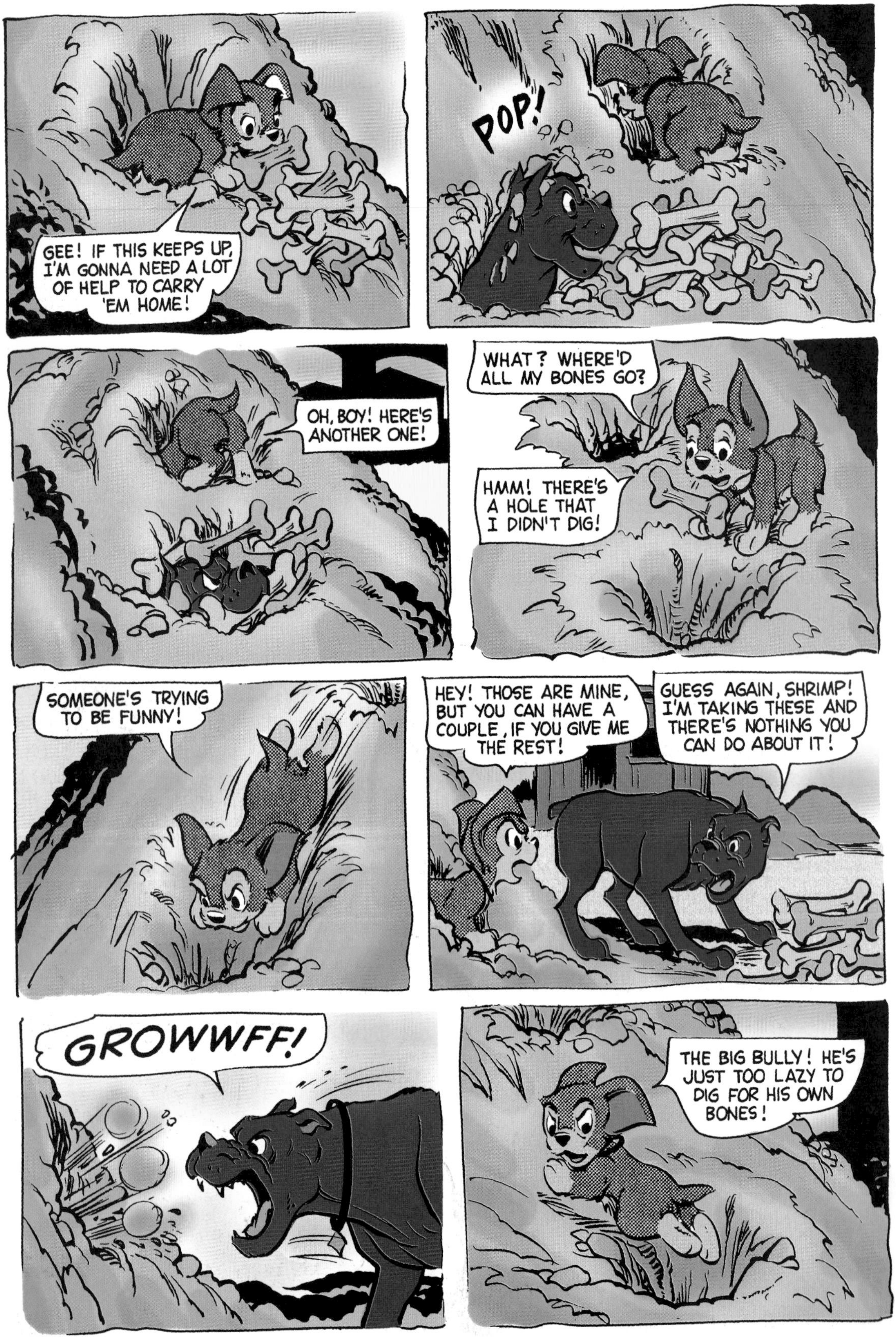
GEE! IF THIS KEEPS UP, I'M GONNA NEED A LOT OF HELP TO CARRY 'EM HOME!
POP!
OH, BOY! HERE'S ANOTHER ONE!
WHAT? WHERE'D ALL MY BONES GO?
HMM! THERE'S A HOLE THAT I DIDN'T DIG!
SOMEONE'S TRYING TO BE FUNNY!
HEY! THOSE ARE MINE, BUT YOU CAN HAVE A COUPLE, IF YOU GIVE ME THE REST!
GUESS AGAIN, SHRIMP! I'M TAKING THESE AND THERE'S NOTHING YOU CAN DO ABOUT IT!
GROWWFF!
THE BIG BULLY! HE'S JUST TOO LAZY TO DIG FOR HIS OWN BONES!

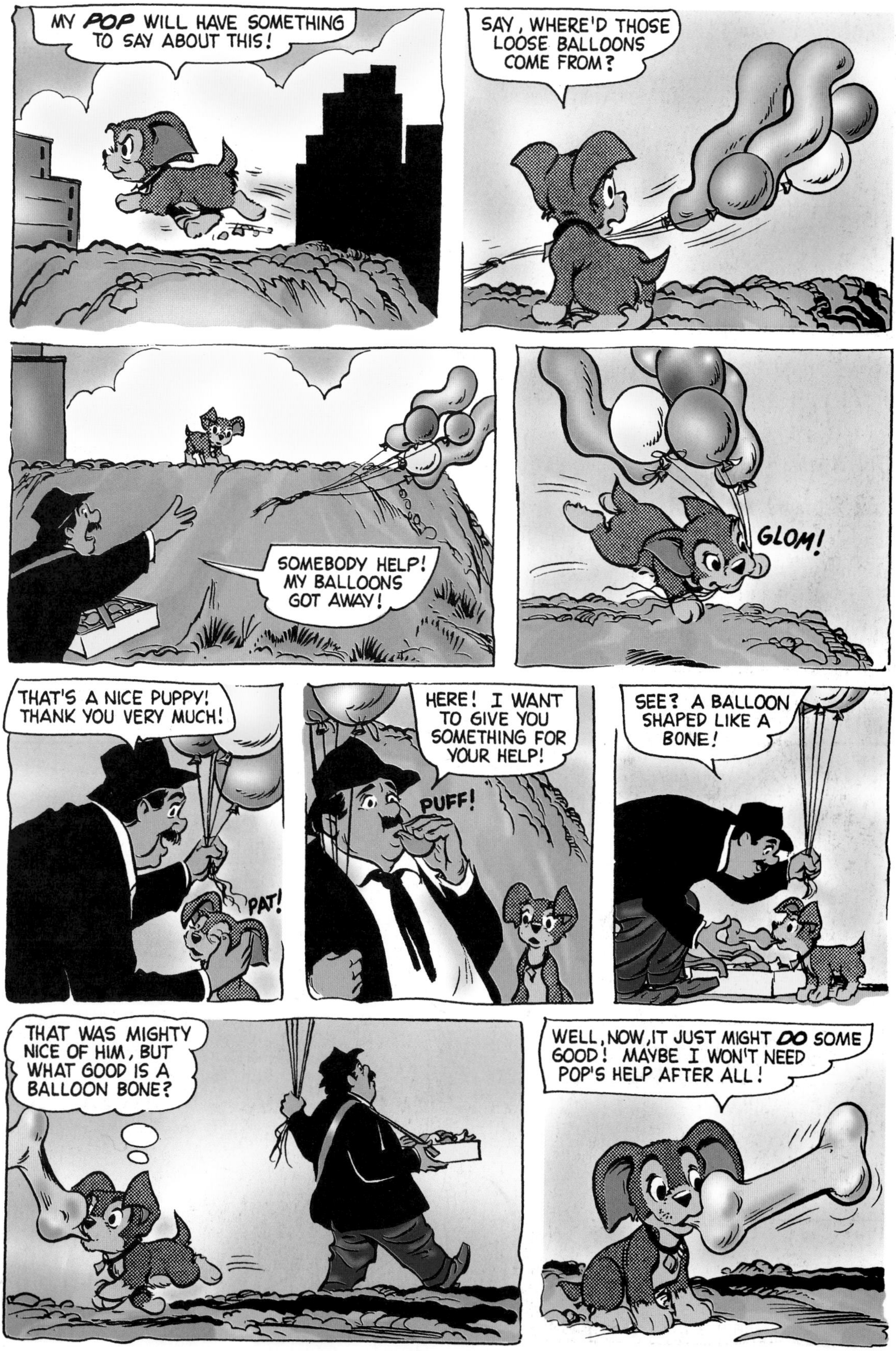
MY POP WILL HAVE SOMETHING TO SAY ABOUT THIS!
SAY, WHERE'D THOSE LOOSE BALLOONS COME FROM?
SOMEBODY HELP! MY BALLOONS GOT AWAY!
GLOM!
THAT'S A NICE PUPPY! THANK YOU VERY MUCH!
PAT!
HERE! I WANT TO GIVE YOU SOMETHING FOR YOUR HELP!
PUFF!
SEE? A BALLOON SHAPED LIKE A BONE!
THAT WAS MIGHTY NICE OF HIM, BUT WHAT GOOD IS A BALLOON BONE?
WELL, NOW, IT JUST MIGHT DO SOME GOOD! MAYBE I WON'T NEED POP'S HELP AFTER ALL!

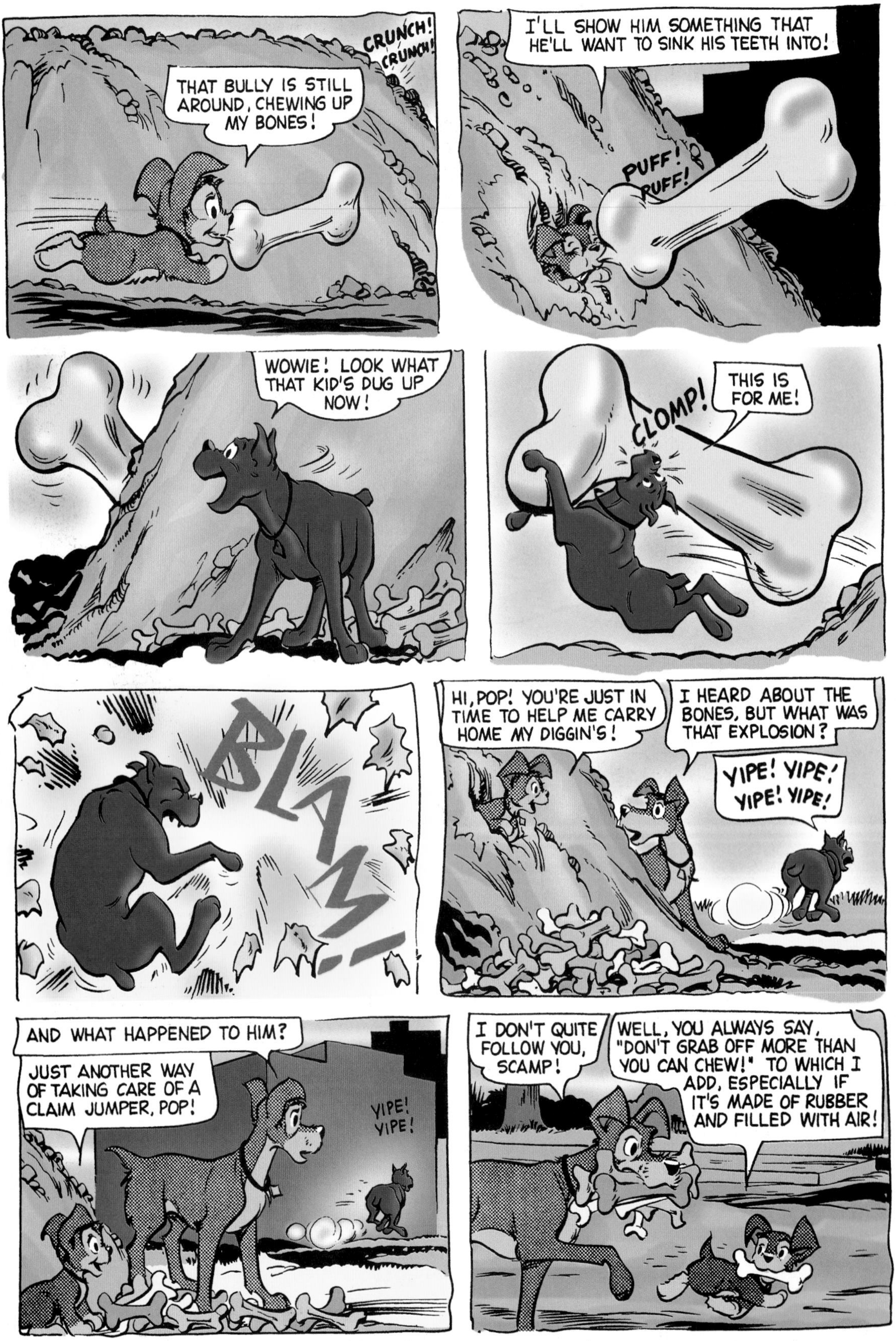
CRUNCH! CRUNCH!
THAT BULLY IS STILL AROUND, CHEWING UP MY BONES!
I'LL SHOW HIM SOMETHING THAT HE'LL WANT TO SINK HIS TEETH INTO!
PUFF! PUFF!
WOWIE! LOOK WHAT THAT KID'S DUG UP NOW!
CLOMP!
THIS IS FOR ME!
BLAM!
HI, POP! YOU'RE JUST IN TIME TO HELP ME CARRY HOME MY DIGGIN'S!
I HEARD ABOUT THE BONES, BUT WHAT WAS THAT EXPLOSION?
YIPE! YIPE! YIPE! YIPE!
AND WHAT HAPPENED TO HIM?
JUST ANOTHER WAY OF TAKING CARE OF A CLAIM JUMPER, POP!
YIPE! YIPE!
I DON'T QUITE FOLLOW YOU, SCAMP!
WELL, YOU ALWAYS SAY, "DON'T GRAB OFF MORE THAN YOU CAN CHEW!" TO WHICH I ADD, ESPECIALLY IF IT'S MADE OF RUBBER AND FILLED WITH AIR!

GEMSTONE PUBLISHING
presents

YOUR FAVORITE DISNEY COMICS

© 2006 Disney
Enterprises Inc.

Delivered right to your door!

We know how much you enjoy visiting your local comic shop, but wouldn't it be nice to have your favorite
Disney comics delivered to you? Subscribe today and we'll send the latest issues of your favorite comics directly to
your doorstep. And if you would still prefer to browse through the latest in comic art but aren't sure where to go,
check out the Comic Shop Locator Service at www.diamondcomics.com/csls or call 1-888-COMIC-BOOK.

Walt Disney's Donald Duck in Invention Contention

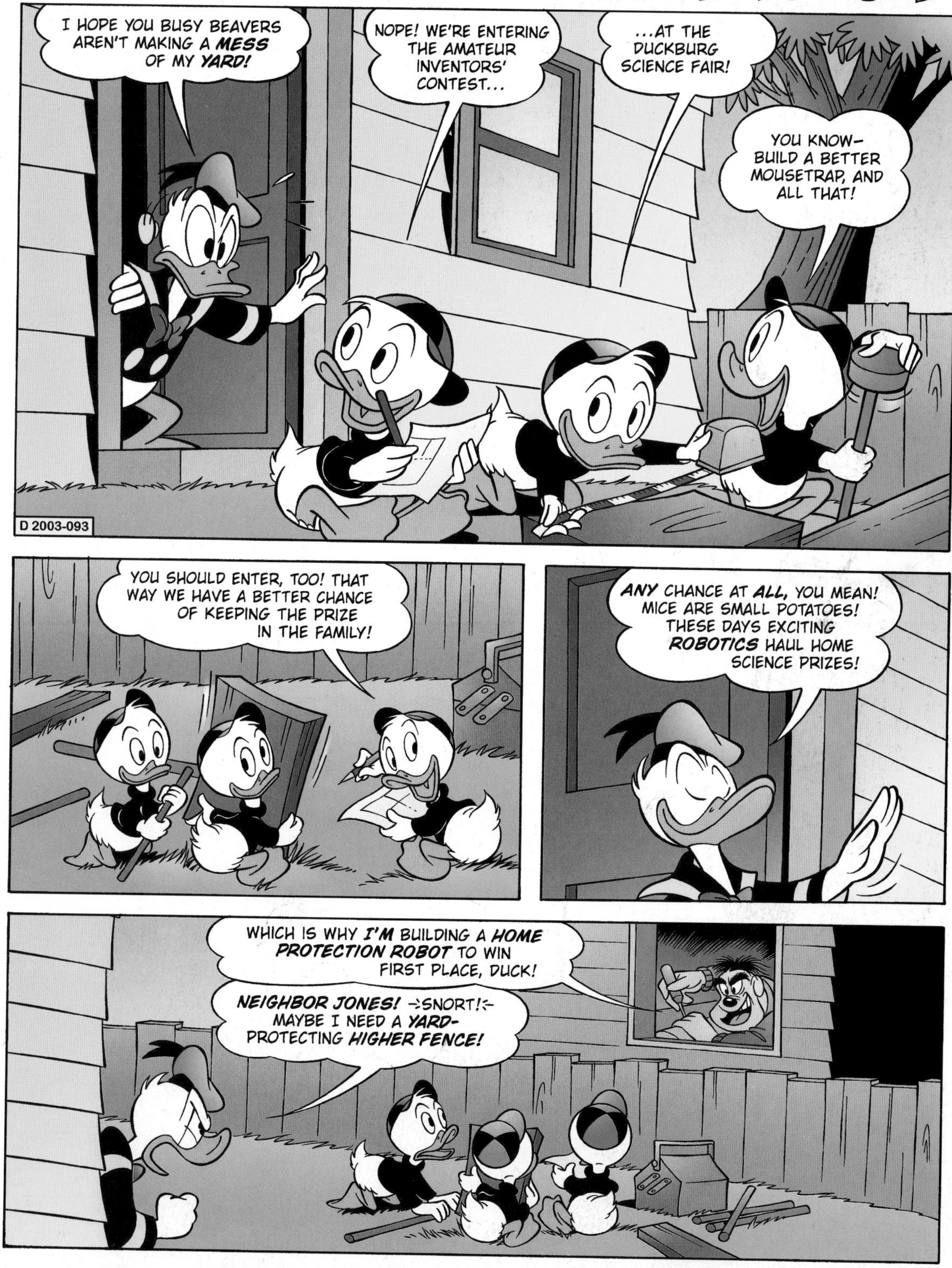

I HOPE YOU BUSY BEAVERS AREN'T MAKING A MESS OF MY YARD!
NOPE! WE'RE ENTERING THE AMATEUR INVENTORS' CONTEST...
...AT THE DUCKBURG SCIENCE FAIR!
YOU KNOW– BUILD A BETTER MOUSETRAP, AND ALL THAT!
D 2003-093
YOU SHOULD ENTER, TOO! THAT WAY WE HAVE A BETTER CHANCE OF KEEPING THE PRIZE IN THE FAMILY!
ANY CHANCE AT ALL, YOU MEAN! MICE ARE SMALL POTATOES! THESE DAYS EXCITING ROBOTICS HAUL HOME SCIENCE PRIZES!
WHICH IS WHY I'M BUILDING A HOME PROTECTION ROBOT TO WIN FIRST PLACE, DUCK!
NEIGHBOR JONES! -SNORT!- MAYBE I NEED A YARD-PROTECTING HIGHER FENCE!

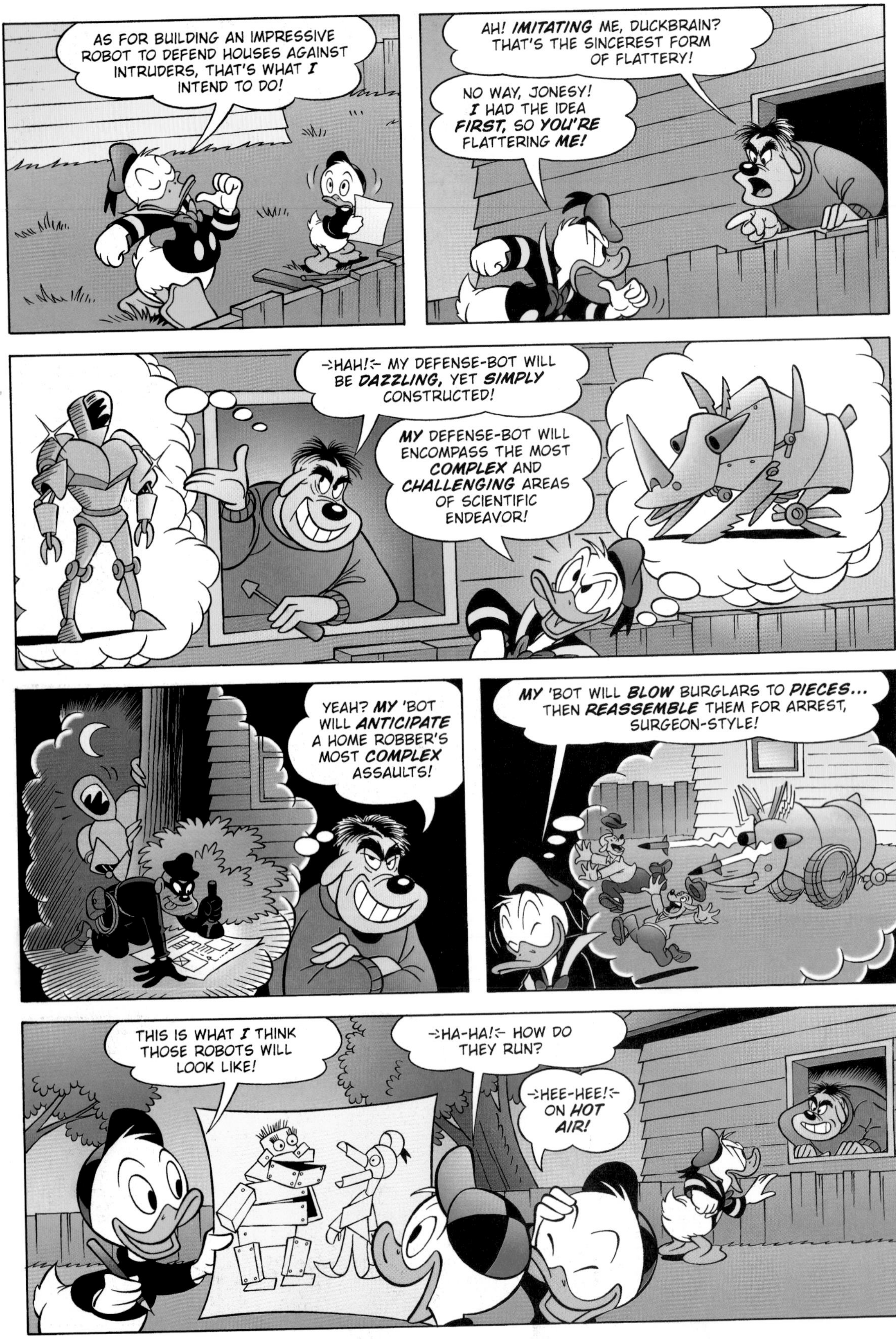
AS FOR BUILDING AN IMPRESSIVE ROBOT TO DEFEND HOUSES AGAINST INTRUDERS, THAT'S WHAT I INTEND TO DO!
AH! IMITATING ME, DUCKBRAIN? THAT'S THE SINCEREST FORM OF FLATTERY!
NO WAY, JONESY! I HAD THE IDEA FIRST, SO YOU'RE FLATTERING ME!
-HAH!- MY DEFENSE-BOT WILL BE DAZZLING, YET SIMPLY CONSTRUCTED!
MY DEFENSE-BOT WILL ENCOMPASS THE MOST COMPLEX AND CHALLENGING AREAS OF SCIENTIFIC ENDEAVOR!
YEAH? MY 'BOT WILL ANTICIPATE A HOME ROBBER'S MOST COMPLEX ASSAULTS!
MY 'BOT WILL BLOW BURGLARS TO PIECES... THEN REASSEMBLE THEM FOR ARREST, SURGEON-STYLE!
THIS IS WHAT I THINK THOSE ROBOTS WILL LOOK LIKE!
-HA-HA!- HOW DO THEY RUN?
-HEE-HEE!- ON HOT AIR!

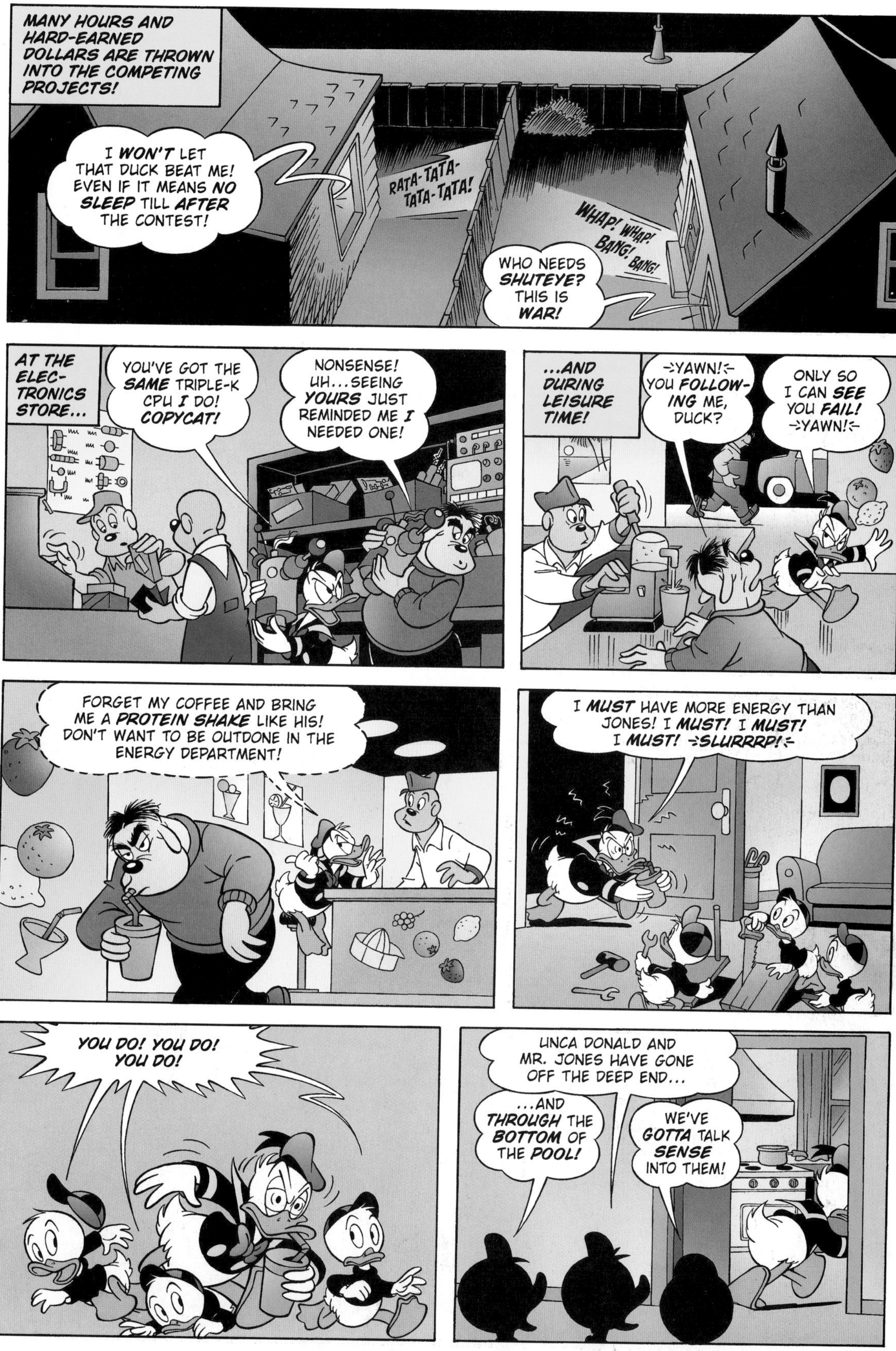
MANY HOURS AND HARD-EARNED DOLLARS ARE THROWN INTO THE COMPETING PROJECTS!
I WON'T LET THAT DUCK BEAT ME! EVEN IF IT MEANS NO SLEEP TILL AFTER THE CONTEST!
RATA-TATA-TATA-TATA!
WHAP! WHAP! BANG! BANG!
WHO NEEDS SHUTEYE? THIS IS WAR!
AT THE ELECTRONICS STORE...
YOU'VE GOT THE SAME TRIPLE-K CPU I DO! COPYCAT!
NONSENSE! UH...SEEING YOURS JUST REMINDED ME I NEEDED ONE!
...AND DURING LEISURE TIME!
-YAWN!- YOU FOLLOWING ME, DUCK?
ONLY SO I CAN SEE YOU FAIL! -YAWN!-
FORGET MY COFFEE AND BRING ME A PROTEIN SHAKE LIKE HIS! DON'T WANT TO BE OUTDONE IN THE ENERGY DEPARTMENT!
I MUST HAVE MORE ENERGY THAN JONES! I MUST! I MUST! I MUST! -SLURRRP!-
YOU DO! YOU DO! YOU DO!
UNCA DONALD AND MR. JONES HAVE GONE OFF THE DEEP END...
...AND THROUGH THE BOTTOM OF THE POOL!
WE'VE GOTTA TALK SENSE INTO THEM!

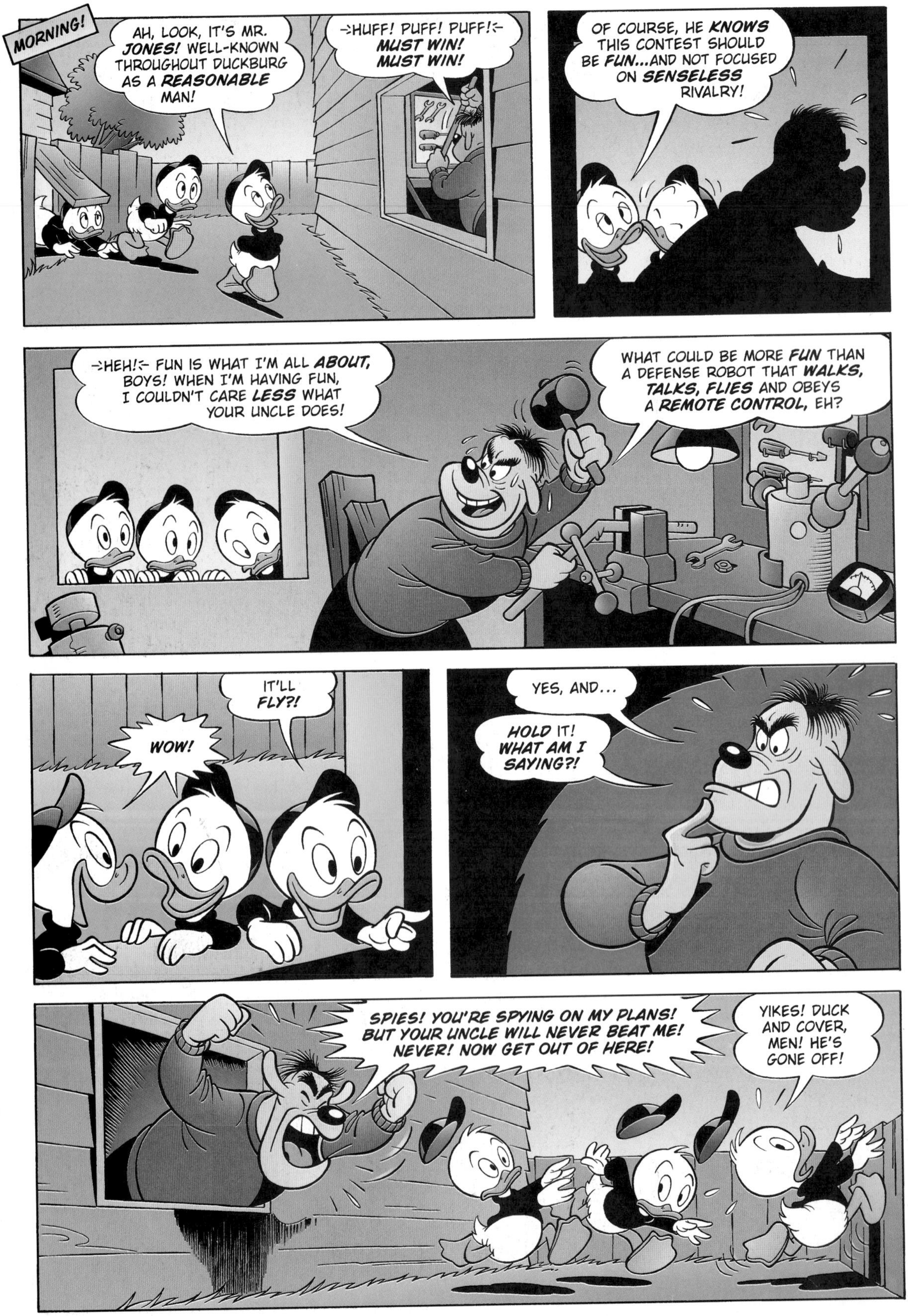
MORNING!
AH, LOOK, IT'S MR. JONES! WELL-KNOWN THROUGHOUT DUCKBURG AS A REASONABLE MAN!
–HUFF! PUFF! PUFF!– MUST WIN! MUST WIN!
OF COURSE, HE KNOWS THIS CONTEST SHOULD BE FUN...AND NOT FOCUSED ON SENSELESS RIVALRY!
–HEH!– FUN IS WHAT I'M ALL ABOUT, BOYS! WHEN I'M HAVING FUN, I COULDN'T CARE LESS WHAT YOUR UNCLE DOES!
WHAT COULD BE MORE FUN THAN A DEFENSE ROBOT THAT WALKS, TALKS, FLIES AND OBEYS A REMOTE CONTROL, EH?
WOW!
IT'LL FLY?!
YES, AND...
HOLD IT! WHAT AM I SAYING?!
SPIES! YOU'RE SPYING ON MY PLANS! BUT YOUR UNCLE WILL NEVER BEAT ME! NEVER! NOW GET OUT OF HERE!
YIKES! DUCK AND COVER, MEN! HE'S GONE OFF!

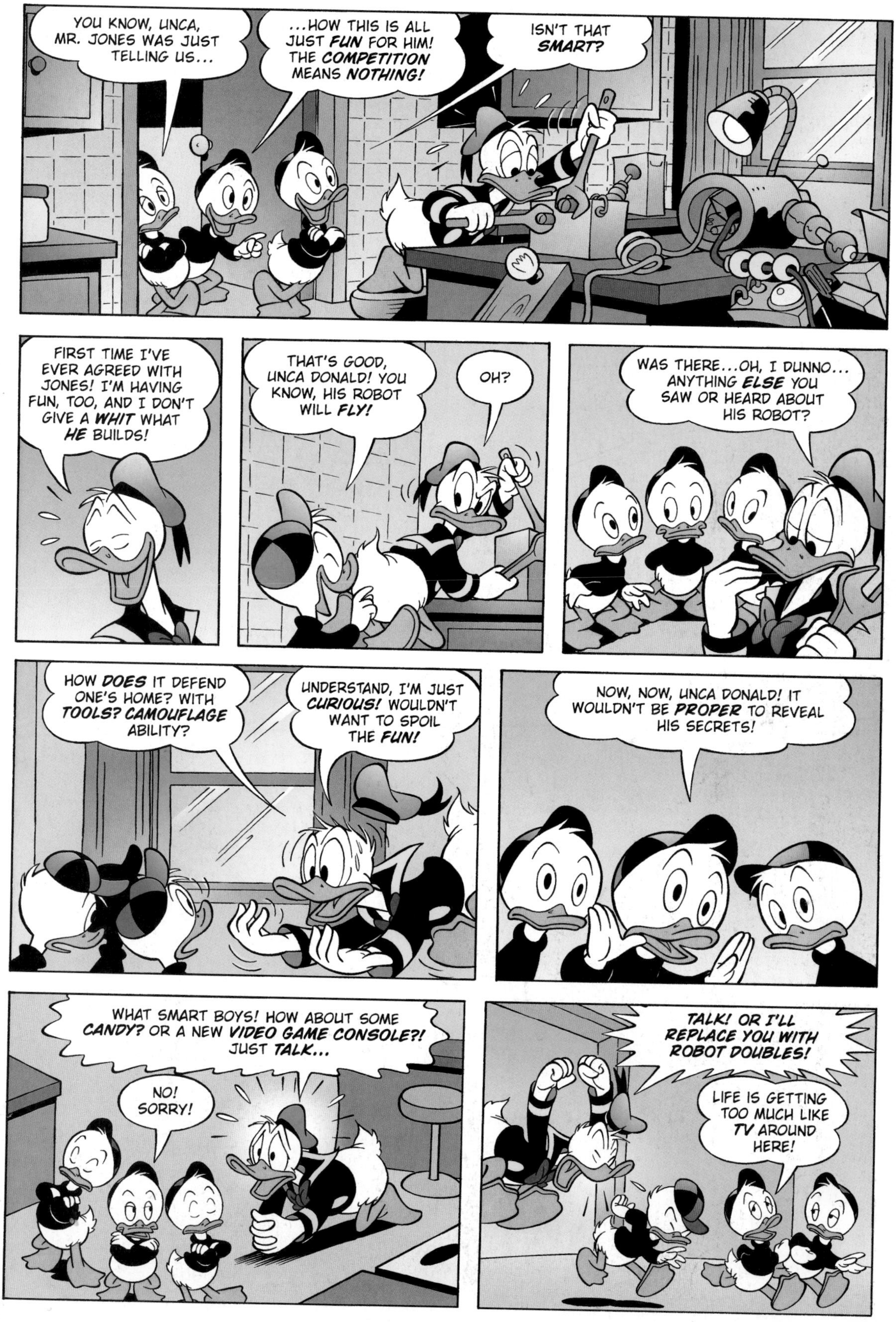
YOU KNOW, UNCA, MR. JONES WAS JUST TELLING US...
...HOW THIS IS ALL JUST FUN FOR HIM! THE COMPETITION MEANS NOTHING!
ISN'T THAT SMART?
FIRST TIME I'VE EVER AGREED WITH JONES! I'M HAVING FUN, TOO, AND I DON'T GIVE A WHIT WHAT HE BUILDS!
THAT'S GOOD, UNCA DONALD! YOU KNOW, HIS ROBOT WILL FLY!
OH?
WAS THERE...OH, I DUNNO... ANYTHING ELSE YOU SAW OR HEARD ABOUT HIS ROBOT?
HOW DOES IT DEFEND ONE'S HOME? WITH TOOLS? CAMOUFLAGE ABILITY?
UNDERSTAND, I'M JUST CURIOUS! WOULDN'T WANT TO SPOIL THE FUN!
NOW, NOW, UNCA DONALD! IT WOULDN'T BE PROPER TO REVEAL HIS SECRETS!
WHAT SMART BOYS! HOW ABOUT SOME CANDY? OR A NEW VIDEO GAME CONSOLE?! JUST TALK...
NO! SORRY!
TALK! OR I'LL REPLACE YOU WITH ROBOT DOUBLES!
LIFE IS GETTING TOO MUCH LIKE TV AROUND HERE!

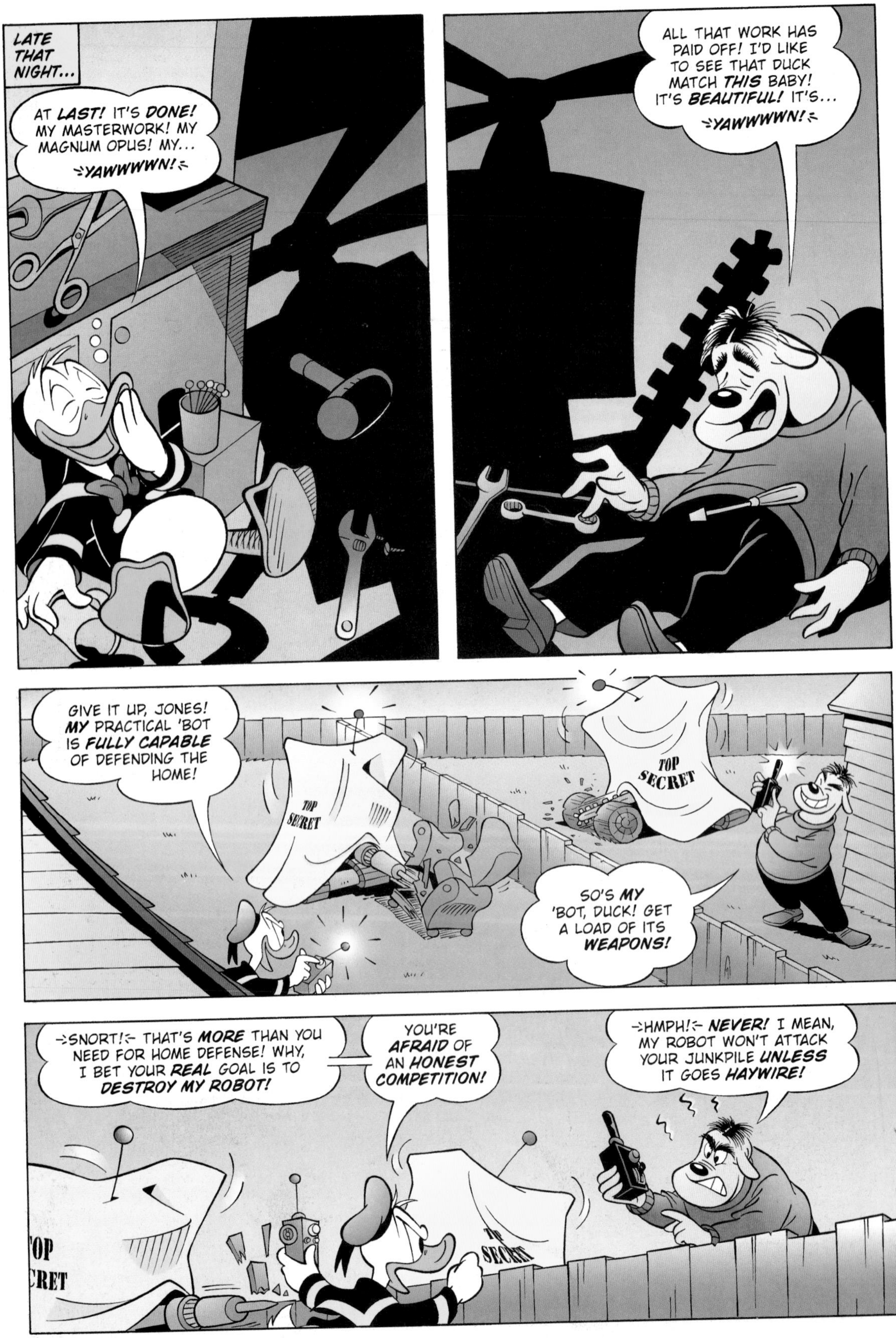
LATE THAT NIGHT...
AT LAST! IT'S DONE! MY MASTERWORK! MY MAGNUM OPUS! MY...
YAWWWWN!
ALL THAT WORK HAS PAID OFF! I'D LIKE TO SEE THAT DUCK MATCH THIS BABY! IT'S BEAUTIFUL! IT'S...
YAWWWWN!
GIVE IT UP, JONES! MY PRACTICAL 'BOT IS FULLY CAPABLE OF DEFENDING THE HOME!
TOP SECRET
TOP SECRET
SO'S MY 'BOT, DUCK! GET A LOAD OF ITS WEAPONS!
SNORT! THAT'S MORE THAN YOU NEED FOR HOME DEFENSE! WHY, I BET YOUR REAL GOAL IS TO DESTROY MY ROBOT!
YOU'RE AFRAID OF AN HONEST COMPETITION!
HMPH! NEVER! I MEAN, MY ROBOT WON'T ATTACK YOUR JUNKPILE UNLESS IT GOES HAYWIRE!

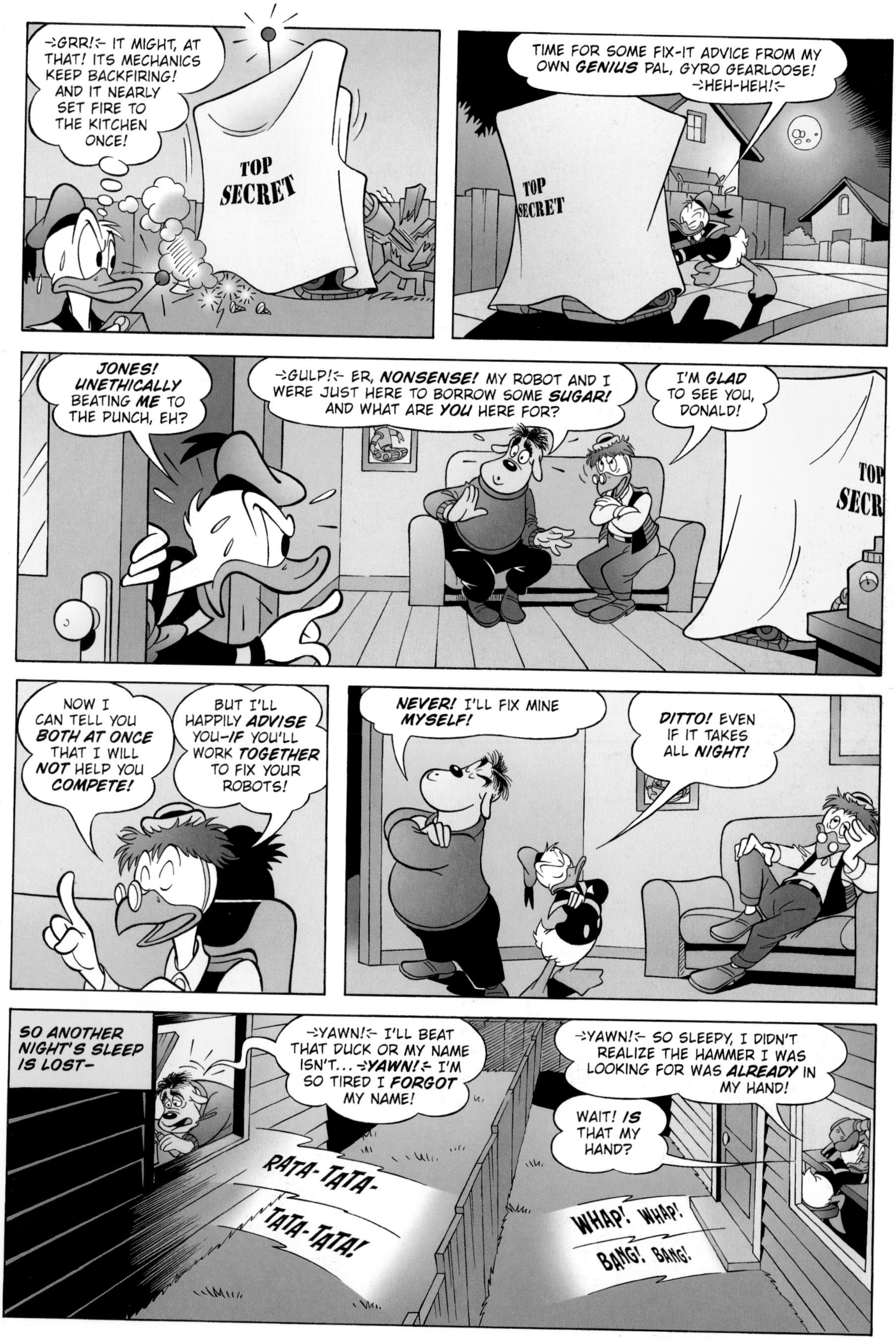
→GRR!← IT MIGHT, AT THAT! ITS MECHANICS KEEP BACKFIRING! AND IT NEARLY SET FIRE TO THE KITCHEN ONCE!
TOP SECRET
TIME FOR SOME FIX-IT ADVICE FROM MY OWN GENIUS PAL, GYRO GEARLOOSE! →HEH-HEH!←
TOP SECRET
JONES! UNETHICALLY BEATING ME TO THE PUNCH, EH?
→GULP!← ER, NONSENSE! MY ROBOT AND I WERE JUST HERE TO BORROW SOME SUGAR! AND WHAT ARE YOU HERE FOR?
I'M GLAD TO SEE YOU, DONALD!
NOW I CAN TELL YOU BOTH AT ONCE THAT I WILL NOT HELP YOU COMPETE!
BUT I'LL HAPPILY ADVISE YOU—IF YOU'LL WORK TOGETHER TO FIX YOUR ROBOTS!
NEVER! I'LL FIX MINE MYSELF!
DITTO! EVEN IF IT TAKES ALL NIGHT!
SO ANOTHER NIGHT'S SLEEP IS LOST—
→YAWN!← I'LL BEAT THAT DUCK OR MY NAME ISN'T... →YAWN!← I'M SO TIRED I FORGOT MY NAME!
→YAWN!← SO SLEEPY, I DIDN'T REALIZE THE HAMMER I WAS LOOKING FOR WAS ALREADY IN MY HAND!
WAIT! IS THAT MY HAND?
RATA-TATA-
TATA-TATA!
WHAP! WHAP!
BANG! BANG!

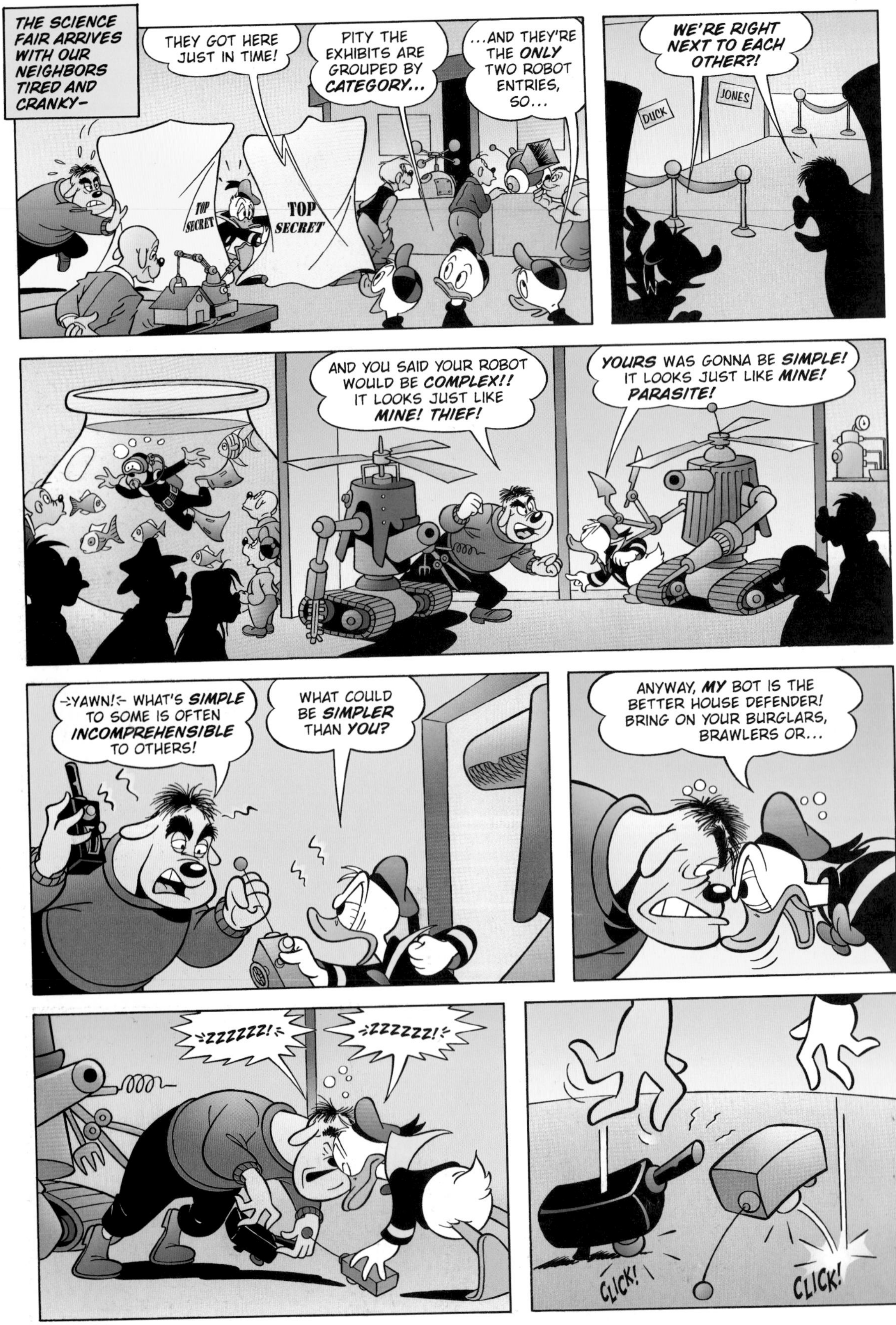
THE SCIENCE FAIR ARRIVES WITH OUR NEIGHBORS TIRED AND CRANKY–
THEY GOT HERE JUST IN TIME!
PITY THE EXHIBITS ARE GROUPED BY CATEGORY...
...AND THEY'RE THE ONLY TWO ROBOT ENTRIES, SO...
TOP SECRET
TOP SECRET
WE'RE RIGHT NEXT TO EACH OTHER?!
DUCK
JONES
AND YOU SAID YOUR ROBOT WOULD BE COMPLEX!! IT LOOKS JUST LIKE MINE! THIEF!
YOURS WAS GONNA BE SIMPLE! IT LOOKS JUST LIKE MINE! PARASITE!
–YAWN!– WHAT'S SIMPLE TO SOME IS OFTEN INCOMPREHENSIBLE TO OTHERS!
WHAT COULD BE SIMPLER THAN YOU?
ANYWAY, MY BOT IS THE BETTER HOUSE DEFENDER! BRING ON YOUR BURGLARS, BRAWLERS OR...
ZZZZZZ!
ZZZZZZ!
CLICK!
CLICK!

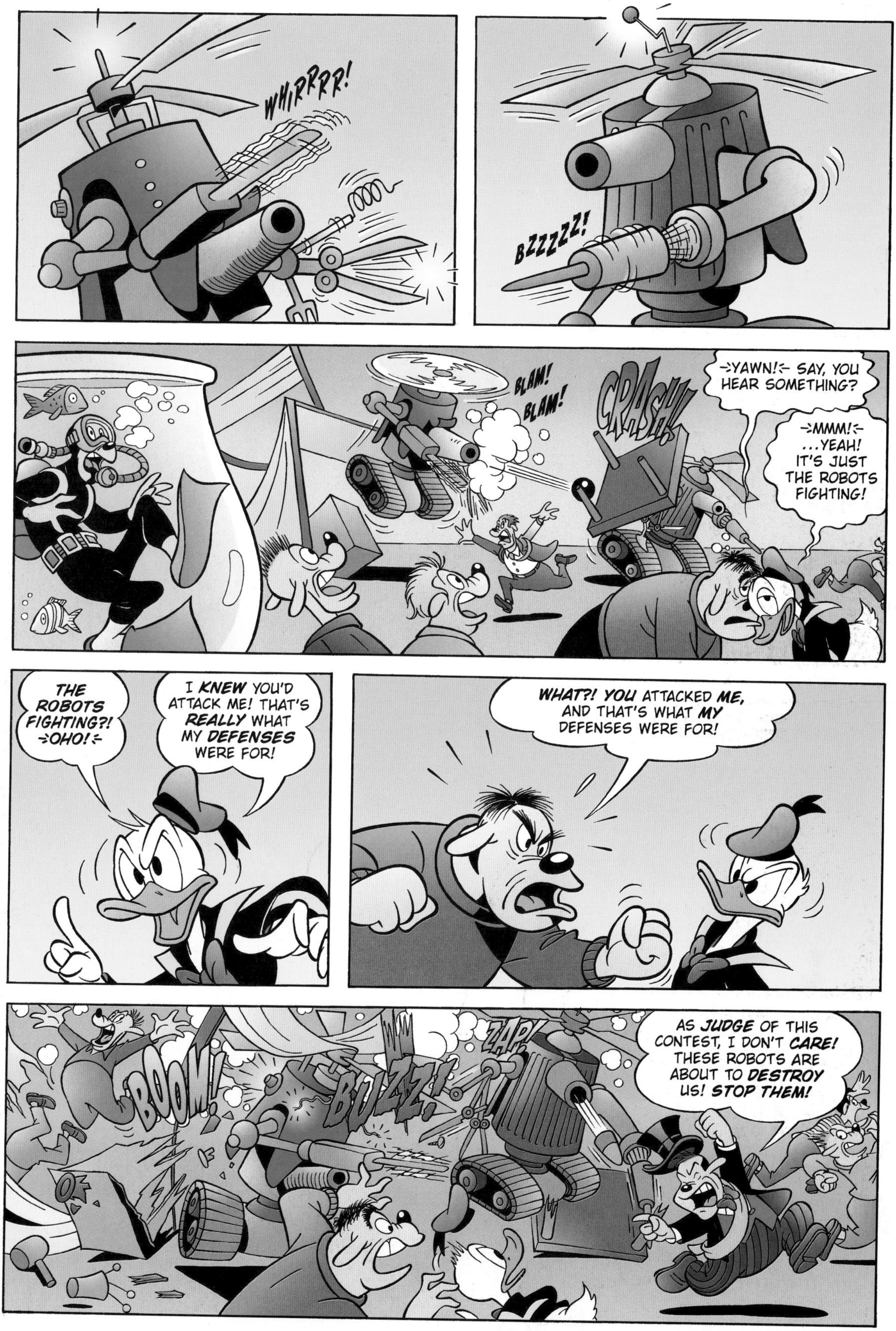
WHIRRRR!
BZZZZZ!
BLAM! BLAM!
CRASH!
-YAWN!- SAY, YOU HEAR SOMETHING?
-MMM!- ...YEAH! IT'S JUST THE ROBOTS FIGHTING!
THE ROBOTS FIGHTING?! -OHO!-
I KNEW YOU'D ATTACK ME! THAT'S REALLY WHAT MY DEFENSES WERE FOR!
WHAT?! YOU ATTACKED ME, AND THAT'S WHAT MY DEFENSES WERE FOR!
BOOM!
BUZZ!
ZAP!
AS JUDGE OF THIS CONTEST, I DON'T CARE! THESE ROBOTS ARE ABOUT TO DESTROY US! STOP THEM!

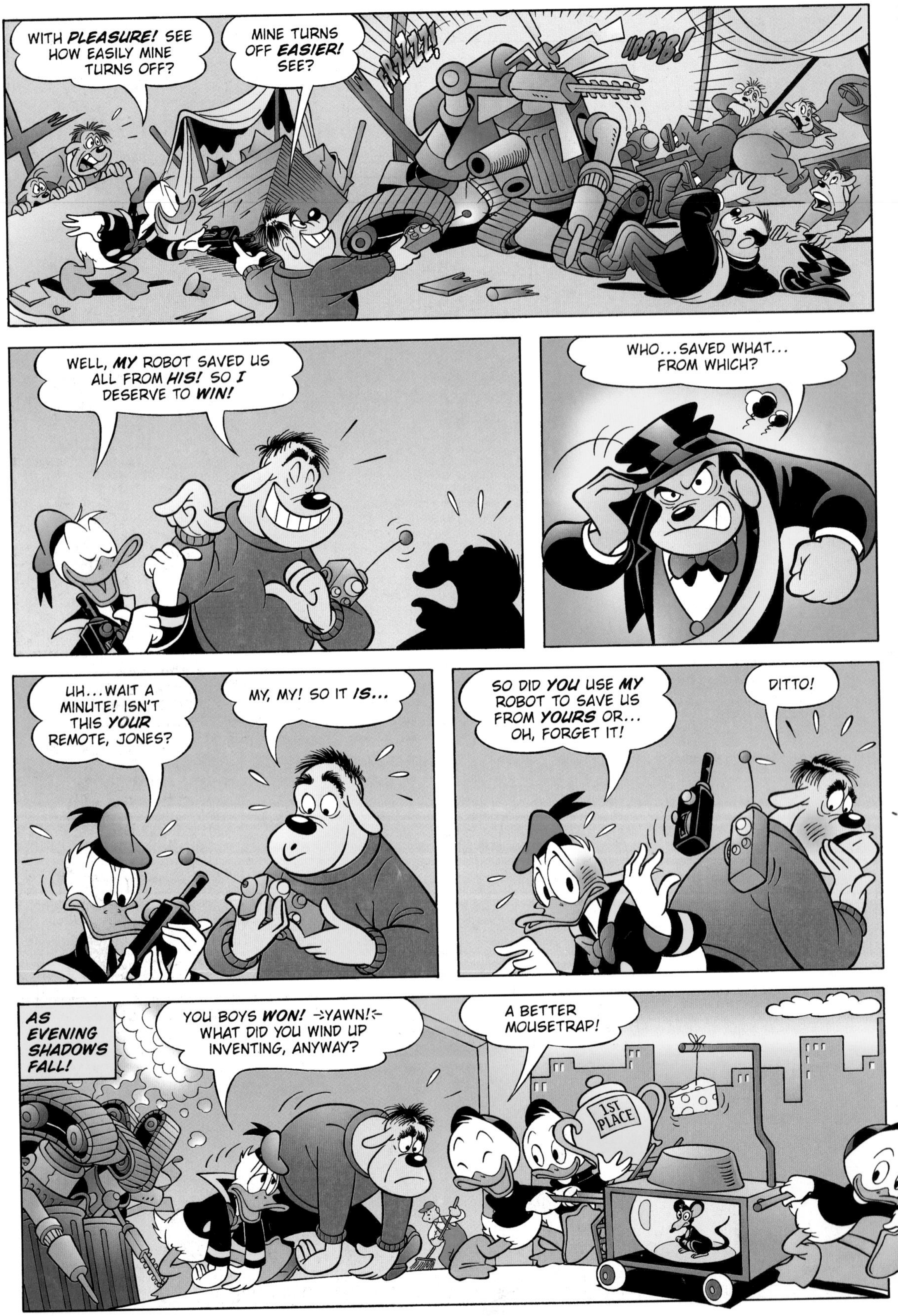
WITH PLEASURE! SEE HOW EASILY MINE TURNS OFF?
MINE TURNS OFF EASIER! SEE?
FRZZZZZ!
URBBB!
WELL, MY ROBOT SAVED US ALL FROM HIS! SO I DESERVE TO WIN!
WHO...SAVED WHAT... FROM WHICH?
UH...WAIT A MINUTE! ISN'T THIS YOUR REMOTE, JONES?
MY, MY! SO IT IS...
SO DID YOU USE MY ROBOT TO SAVE US FROM YOURS OR... OH, FORGET IT!
DITTO!
AS EVENING SHADOWS FALL!
YOU BOYS WON! →YAWN!← WHAT DID YOU WIND UP INVENTING, ANYWAY?
A BETTER MOUSETRAP!
1ST PLACE

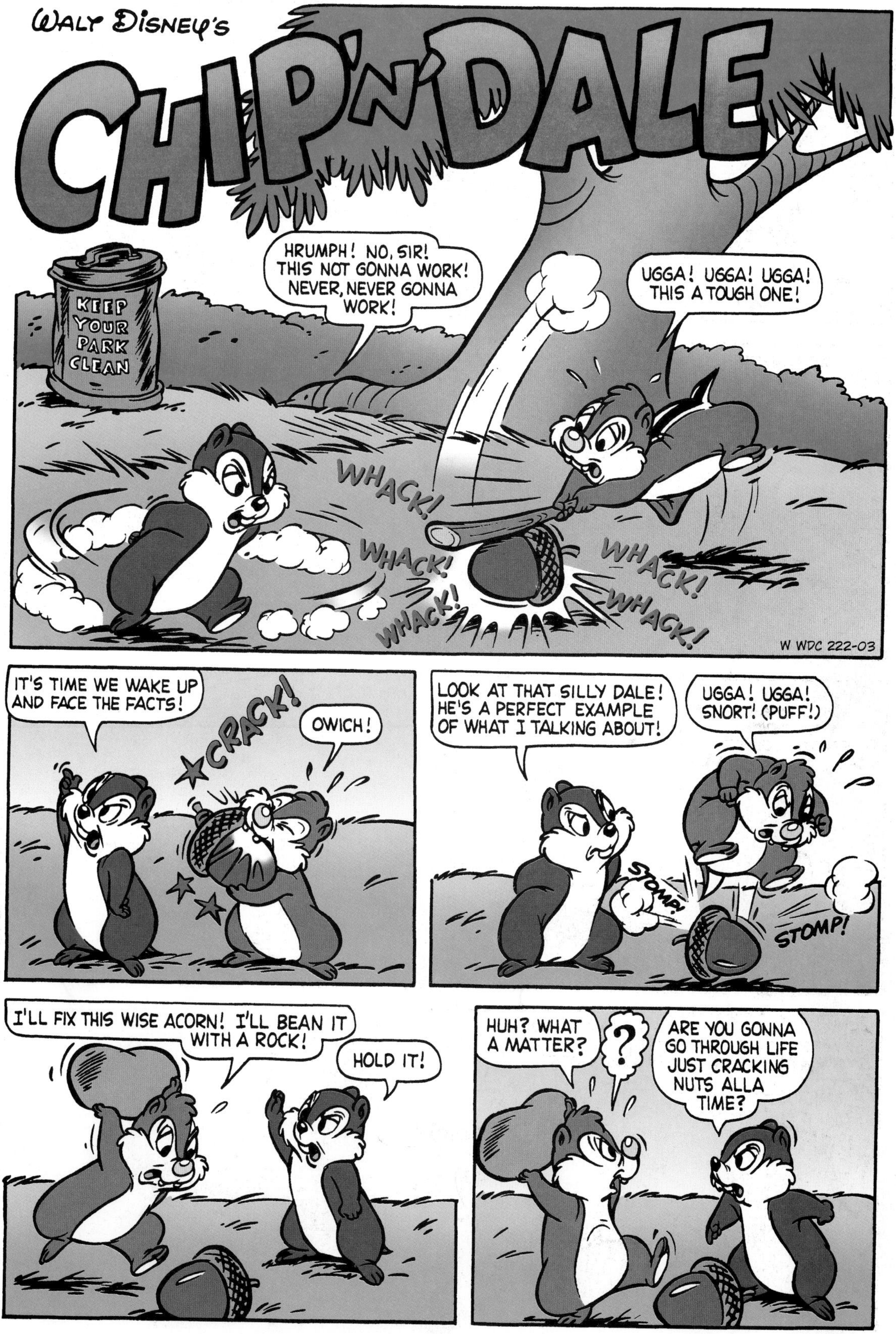
WALT DISNEY'S
CHIP 'N' DALE
KEEP YOUR PARK CLEAN
HRUMPH! NO, SIR! THIS NOT GONNA WORK! NEVER, NEVER GONNA WORK!
UGGA! UGGA! UGGA! THIS A TOUGH ONE!
WHACK! WHACK! WHACK! WHACK! WHACK!
W WDC 222-03
IT'S TIME WE WAKE UP AND FACE THE FACTS!
CRACK!
OWICH!
LOOK AT THAT SILLY DALE! HE'S A PERFECT EXAMPLE OF WHAT I TALKING ABOUT!
UGGA! UGGA! SNORT! (PUFF!)
STOMP!
STOMP!
I'LL FIX THIS WISE ACORN! I'LL BEAN IT WITH A ROCK!
HOLD IT!
HUH? WHAT A MATTER?
?
ARE YOU GONNA GO THROUGH LIFE JUST CRACKING NUTS ALLA TIME?

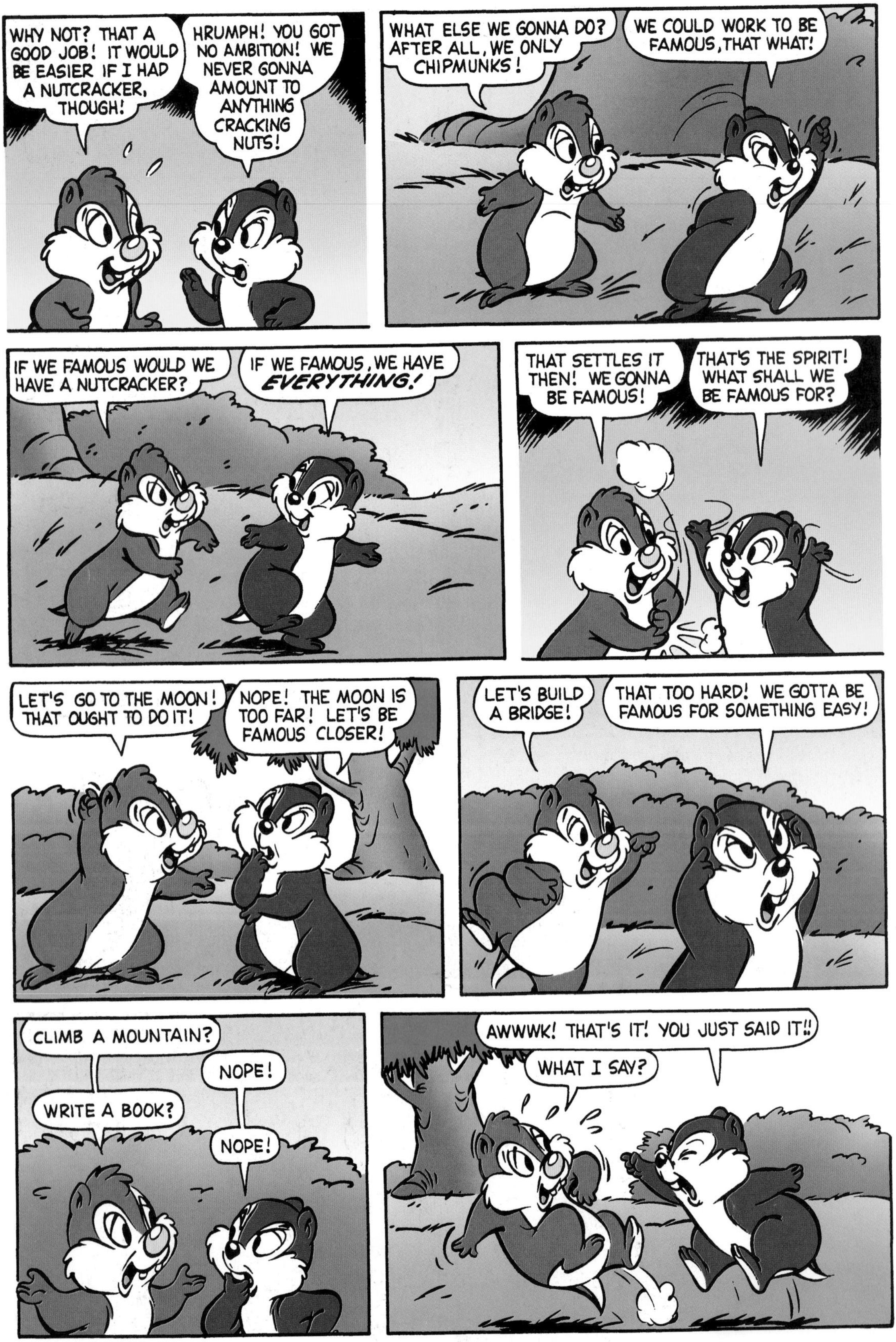
WHY NOT? THAT A GOOD JOB! IT WOULD BE EASIER IF I HAD A NUTCRACKER, THOUGH!
HRUMPH! YOU GOT NO AMBITION! WE NEVER GONNA AMOUNT TO ANYTHING CRACKING NUTS!
WHAT ELSE WE GONNA DO? AFTER ALL, WE ONLY CHIPMUNKS!
WE COULD WORK TO BE FAMOUS, THAT WHAT!
IF WE FAMOUS WOULD WE HAVE A NUTCRACKER?
IF WE FAMOUS, WE HAVE EVERYTHING!
THAT SETTLES IT THEN! WE GONNA BE FAMOUS!
THAT'S THE SPIRIT! WHAT SHALL WE BE FAMOUS FOR?
LET'S GO TO THE MOON! THAT OUGHT TO DO IT!
NOPE! THE MOON IS TOO FAR! LET'S BE FAMOUS CLOSER!
LET'S BUILD A BRIDGE!
THAT TOO HARD! WE GOTTA BE FAMOUS FOR SOMETHING EASY!
CLIMB A MOUNTAIN?
NOPE!
WRITE A BOOK?
NOPE!
AWWWK! THAT'S IT! YOU JUST SAID IT!!
WHAT I SAY?

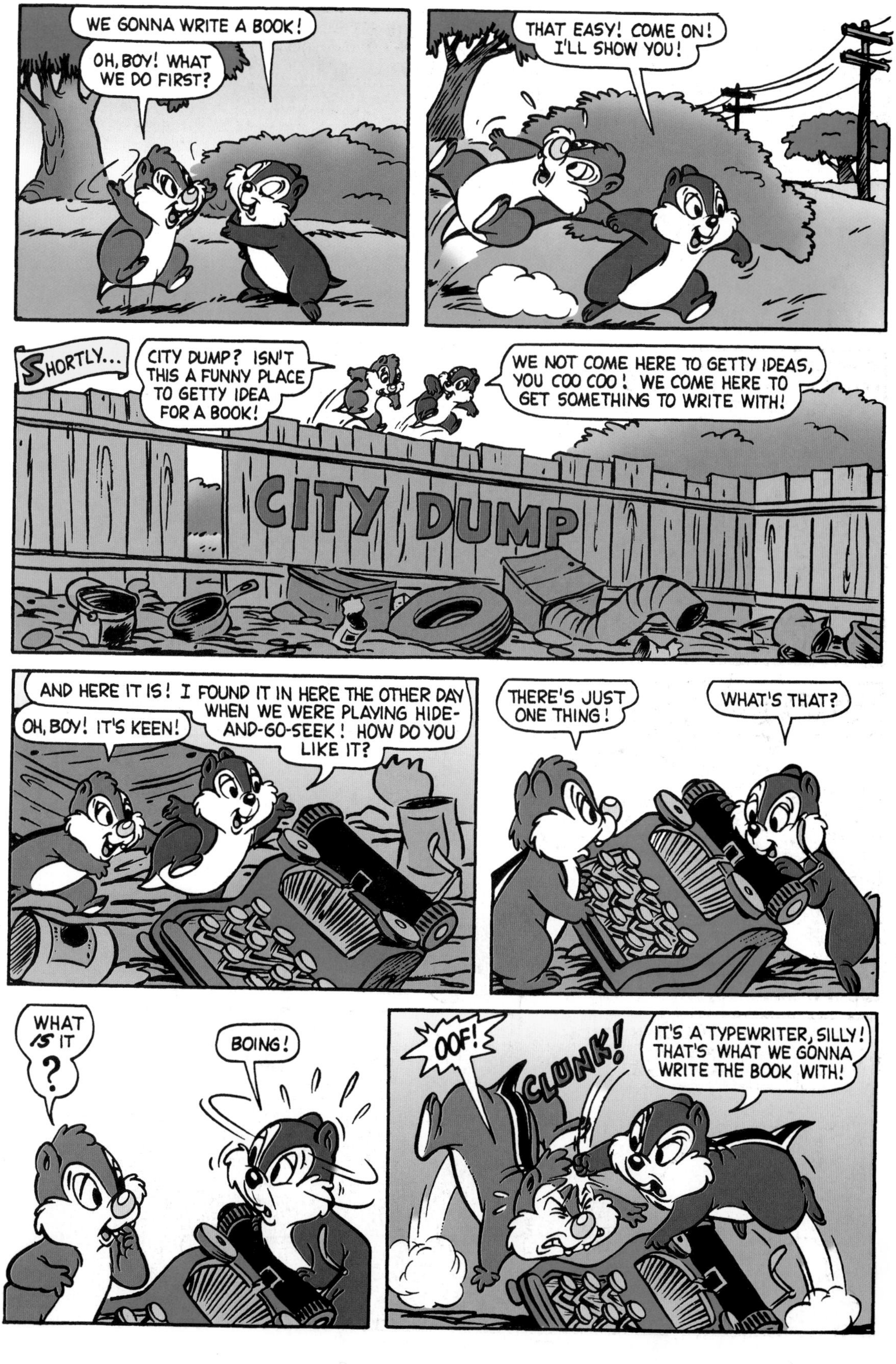
WE GONNA WRITE A BOOK!
OH, BOY! WHAT WE DO FIRST?
THAT EASY! COME ON! I'LL SHOW YOU!
SHORTLY...
CITY DUMP? ISN'T THIS A FUNNY PLACE TO GETTY IDEA FOR A BOOK!
WE NOT COME HERE TO GETTY IDEAS, YOU COO COO! WE COME HERE TO GET SOMETHING TO WRITE WITH!
CITY DUMP
AND HERE IT IS! I FOUND IT IN HERE THE OTHER DAY WHEN WE WERE PLAYING HIDE-AND-GO-SEEK! HOW DO YOU LIKE IT?
OH, BOY! IT'S KEEN!
THERE'S JUST ONE THING!
WHAT'S THAT?
WHAT IS IT ?
BOING!
OOF!
CLUNK!
IT'S A TYPEWRITER, SILLY! THAT'S WHAT WE GONNA WRITE THE BOOK WITH!

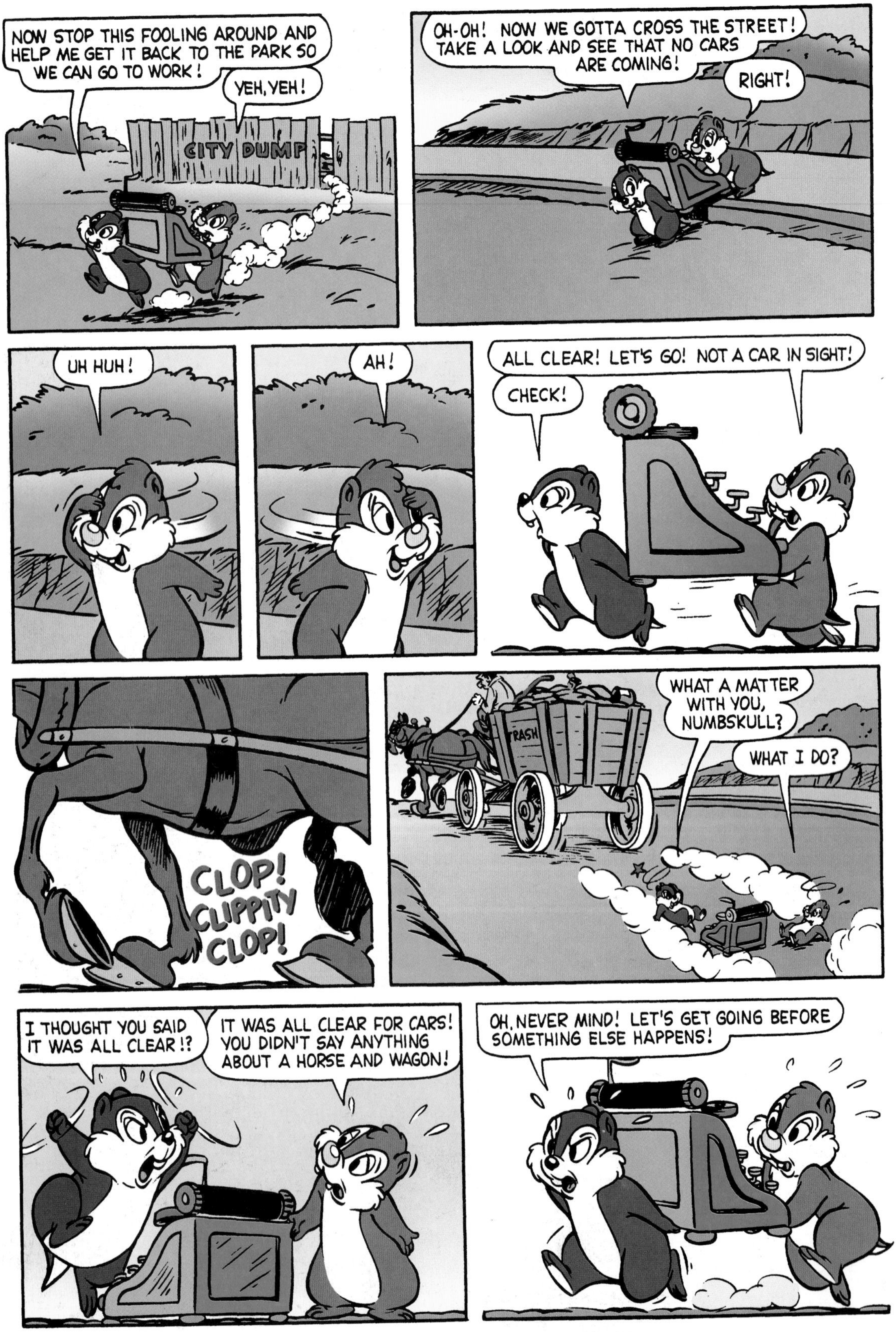
NOW STOP THIS FOOLING AROUND AND HELP ME GET IT BACK TO THE PARK SO WE CAN GO TO WORK!
YEH, YEH!
CITY DUMP
OH-OH! NOW WE GOTTA CROSS THE STREET! TAKE A LOOK AND SEE THAT NO CARS ARE COMING!
RIGHT!
UH HUH!
AH!
ALL CLEAR! LET'S GO! NOT A CAR IN SIGHT!
CHECK!
CLOP! CLIPPITY CLOP!
TRASH
WHAT A MATTER WITH YOU, NUMBSKULL?
WHAT I DO?
I THOUGHT YOU SAID IT WAS ALL CLEAR!?
IT WAS ALL CLEAR FOR CARS! YOU DIDN'T SAY ANYTHING ABOUT A HORSE AND WAGON!
OH, NEVER MIND! LET'S GET GOING BEFORE SOMETHING ELSE HAPPENS!

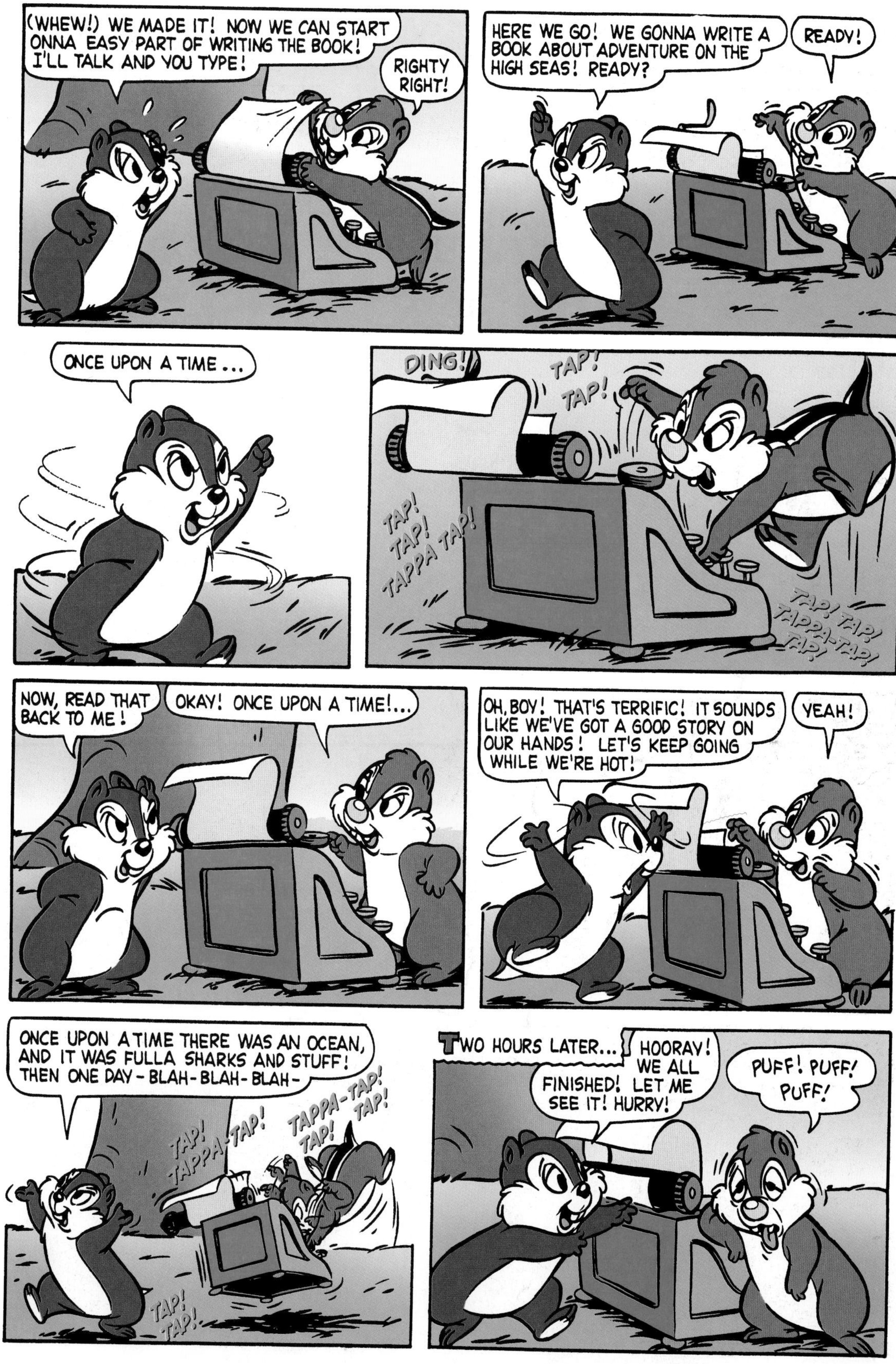
(WHEW!) WE MADE IT! NOW WE CAN START ONNA EASY PART OF WRITING THE BOOK! I'LL TALK AND YOU TYPE!
RIGHTY RIGHT!
HERE WE GO! WE GONNA WRITE A BOOK ABOUT ADVENTURE ON THE HIGH SEAS! READY?
READY!
ONCE UPON A TIME...
DING!
TAP! TAP!
TAP! TAP! TAPPA TAP!
TAP! TAP! TAPPA-TAP! TAP!
NOW, READ THAT BACK TO ME!
OKAY! ONCE UPON A TIME!...
OH, BOY! THAT'S TERRIFIC! IT SOUNDS LIKE WE'VE GOT A GOOD STORY ON OUR HANDS! LET'S KEEP GOING WHILE WE'RE HOT!
YEAH!
ONCE UPON A TIME THERE WAS AN OCEAN, AND IT WAS FULLA SHARKS AND STUFF! THEN ONE DAY - BLAH - BLAH - BLAH -
TAP! TAPPA-TAP!
TAPPA-TAP! TAP! TAP!
TAP! TAP!
TWO HOURS LATER...
HOORAY! WE ALL FINISHED! LET ME SEE IT! HURRY!
PUFF! PUFF! PUFF!

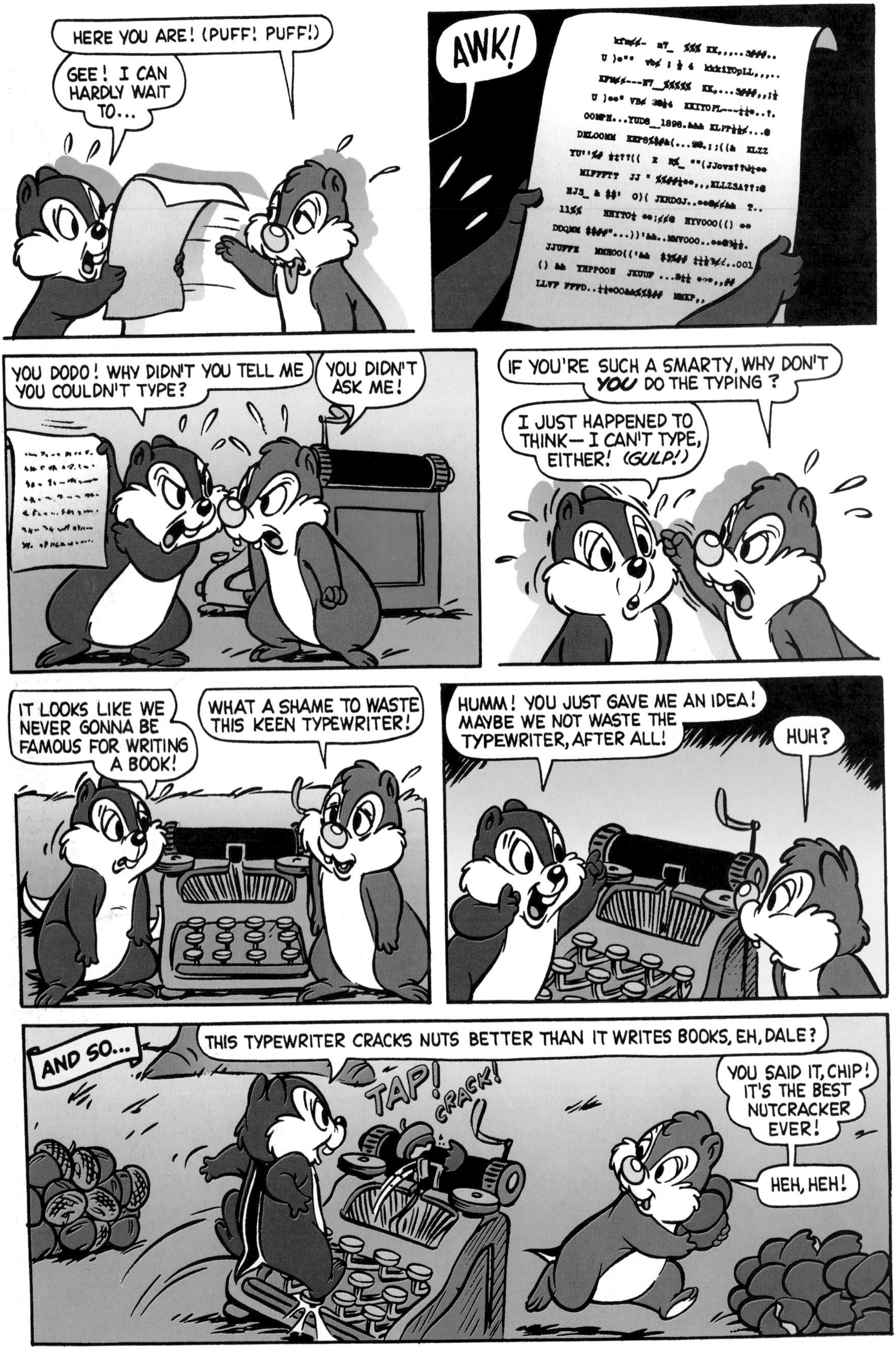
HERE YOU ARE! (PUFF! PUFF!)
GEE! I CAN HARDLY WAIT TO...
AWK!
YOU DODO! WHY DIDN'T YOU TELL ME YOU COULDN'T TYPE?
YOU DIDN'T ASK ME!
IF YOU'RE SUCH A SMARTY, WHY DON'T YOU DO THE TYPING?
I JUST HAPPENED TO THINK—I CAN'T TYPE, EITHER! (GULP!)
IT LOOKS LIKE WE NEVER GONNA BE FAMOUS FOR WRITING A BOOK!
WHAT A SHAME TO WASTE THIS KEEN TYPEWRITER!
HUMM! YOU JUST GAVE ME AN IDEA! MAYBE WE NOT WASTE THE TYPEWRITER, AFTER ALL!
HUH?
AND SO...
THIS TYPEWRITER CRACKS NUTS BETTER THAN IT WRITES BOOKS, EH, DALE?
TAP!
CRACK!
YOU SAID IT, CHIP! IT'S THE BEST NUTCRACKER EVER!
HEH, HEH!

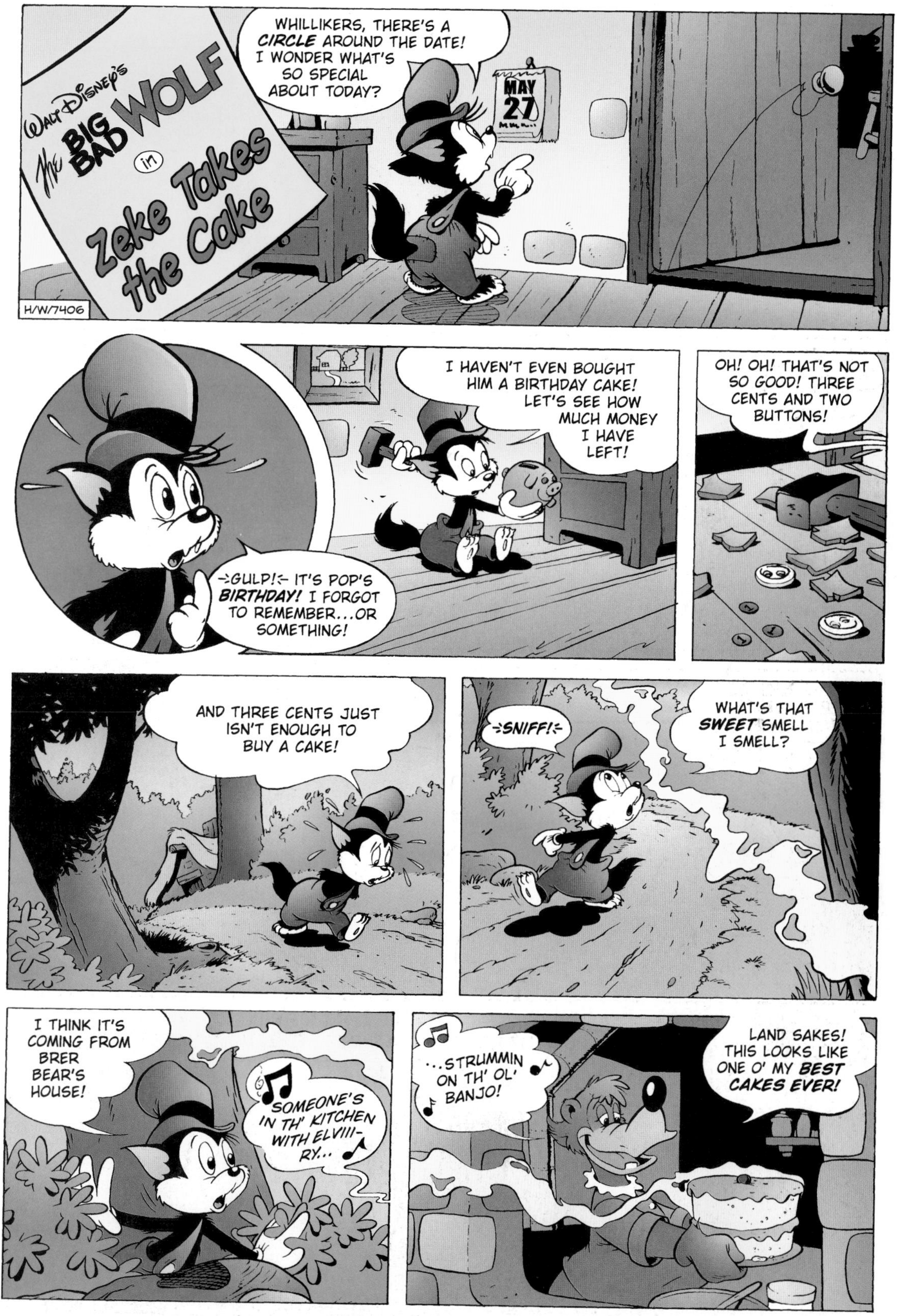
Walt Disney's The Big Bad Wolf in Zeke Takes the Cake
WHILLIKERS, THERE'S A CIRCLE AROUND THE DATE! I WONDER WHAT'S SO SPECIAL ABOUT TODAY?
MAY 27
H/W/7406
-GULP!- IT'S POP'S BIRTHDAY! I FORGOT TO REMEMBER...OR SOMETHING!
I HAVEN'T EVEN BOUGHT HIM A BIRTHDAY CAKE! LET'S SEE HOW MUCH MONEY I HAVE LEFT!
OH! OH! THAT'S NOT SO GOOD! THREE CENTS AND TWO BUTTONS!
AND THREE CENTS JUST ISN'T ENOUGH TO BUY A CAKE!
SNIFF!
WHAT'S THAT SWEET SMELL I SMELL?
I THINK IT'S COMING FROM BRER BEAR'S HOUSE!
SOMEONE'S IN TH' KITCHEN WITH ELVIIII-RY...
...STRUMMIN ON TH' OL' BANJO!
LAND SAKES! THIS LOOKS LIKE ONE O' MY BEST CAKES EVER!

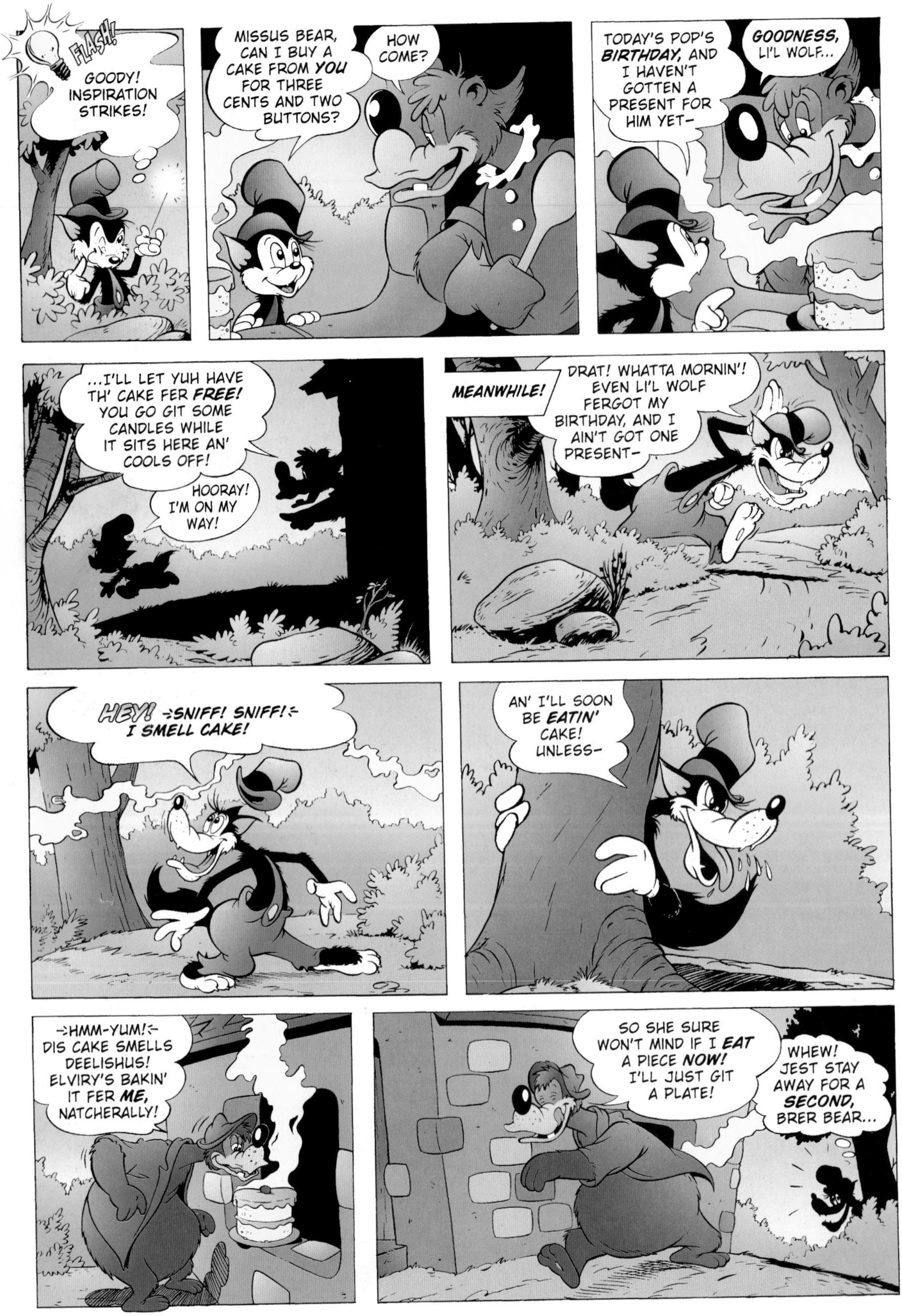
FLASH!
GOODY! INSPIRATION STRIKES!
MISSUS BEAR, CAN I BUY A CAKE FROM YOU FOR THREE CENTS AND TWO BUTTONS?
HOW COME?
TODAY'S POP'S BIRTHDAY, AND I HAVEN'T GOTTEN A PRESENT FOR HIM YET–
GOODNESS, LI'L WOLF...
...I'LL LET YUH HAVE TH' CAKE FER FREE! YOU GO GIT SOME CANDLES WHILE IT SITS HERE AN' COOLS OFF!
HOORAY! I'M ON MY WAY!
MEANWHILE!
DRAT! WHATTA MORNIN'! EVEN LI'L WOLF FERGOT MY BIRTHDAY, AND I AIN'T GOT ONE PRESENT–
HEY! –SNIFF! SNIFF!– I SMELL CAKE!
AN' I'LL SOON BE EATIN' CAKE! UNLESS–
–HMM-YUM!– DIS CAKE SMELLS DEELISHUS! ELVIRY'S BAKIN' IT FER ME, NATCHERALLY!
SO SHE SURE WON'T MIND IF I EAT A PIECE NOW! I'LL JUST GIT A PLATE!
WHEW! JEST STAY AWAY FOR A SECOND, BRER BEAR...

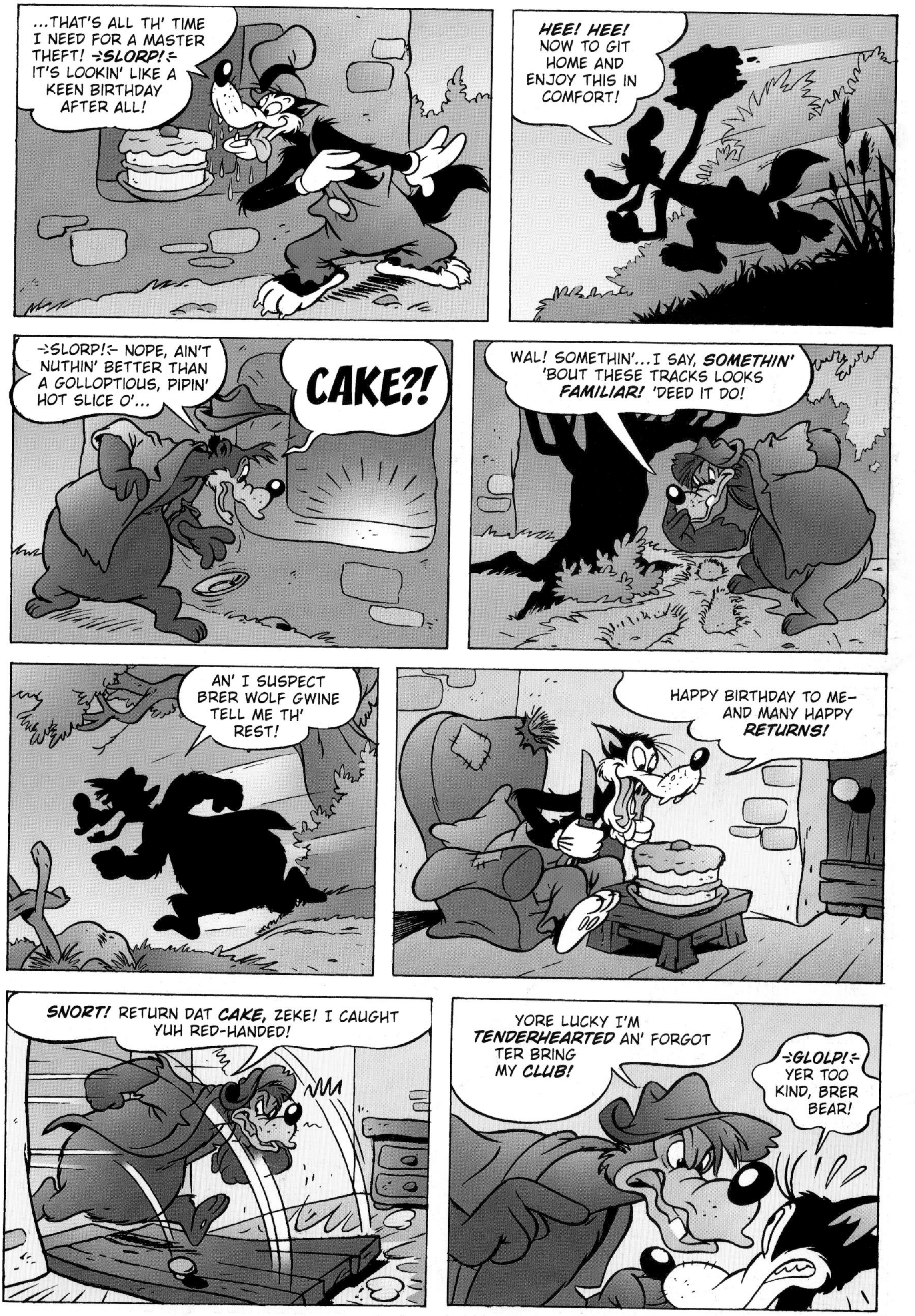
...THAT'S ALL TH' TIME I NEED FOR A MASTER THEFT! -SLORP!- IT'S LOOKIN' LIKE A KEEN BIRTHDAY AFTER ALL!
HEE! HEE! NOW TO GIT HOME AND ENJOY THIS IN COMFORT!
-SLORP!- NOPE, AIN'T NUTHIN' BETTER THAN A GOLLOPTIOUS, PIPIN' HOT SLICE O'...
CAKE?!
WAL! SOMETHIN'...I SAY, SOMETHIN' 'BOUT THESE TRACKS LOOKS FAMILIAR! 'DEED IT DO!
AN' I SUSPECT BRER WOLF GWINE TELL ME TH' REST!
HAPPY BIRTHDAY TO ME— AND MANY HAPPY RETURNS!
SNORT! RETURN DAT CAKE, ZEKE! I CAUGHT YUH RED-HANDED!
YORE LUCKY I'M TENDERHEARTED AN' FORGOT TER BRING MY CLUB!
-GLOLP!- YER TOO KIND, BRER BEAR!

ALL DAT RUNNIN' GAVE ME A *BEAR* OF AN APPETITE FER BAKED GOODS!

DIGGITY DEE! *ORDER* IS *REESTORED!* NOW T' GIT THAT PLATE—

MY, MY, DAT WAS *QUICK!* I SEE TH' CAKE'S COOLED NICELY!

I'LL DELIVER IT TER LI'L WOLF SO'S HE WON'T HAVE TER CARRY IT HIMSELF!

→SIGH!← JUST THINKIN' O' THAT DEELISHUS CAKE MAKES MY MOUTH WATER!

ZEKE'S HOME ALONE! I'LL GIVE IT TER *HIM* THEN!

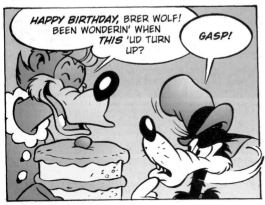

HAPPY BIRTHDAY, BRER WOLF! BEEN WONDERIN' WHEN *THIS* 'UD TURN UP?

GASP!

YEOW! TH' CAKE IS MINE, LONG LIVE TH' CAKE! I'LL TAKE IT INSIDE AN' CHOW DOWN!

MANY HAPPY REETURNS!

YUM!

→SMACK! SMACK!←

MEAN-TIME...

JUMPIN' HOP-FRAWGS! GONE AGIN!

AN' AGIN I GOT A IDEA WHERE TER LOOK! →GRRROWL!←

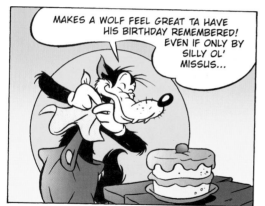

MAKES A WOLF FEEL GREAT TA HAVE HIS BIRTHDAY REMEMBERED! EVEN IF ONLY BY SILLY OL' MISSUS...

AHA! JEST LIKE I FIGGERED!

...BEAR?!

SEE DIS FIST? *I'M GONNER KNOCK...YOUR... HAID...CLEAN...OFF!*

AN' IF I CATCH YUH WID THIS CAKE AGIN, YO' *SPINAL COLUMN* GOES NEXT!

GLORK!

⤐GRUMPH!⤐ NOW I WANT A PIECE O' DIS CAKE MORE'N *EVER!*

WHERE'D I LEAVE MY PLATE? OH WELL, I'LL JUST GIT ME ANOTHER!

IN GO THE CANDLES! PLOP! PLOP!

I CAN'T *WAIT* TO GET THIS HOME! POP WILL BE SO *HAPPY!*

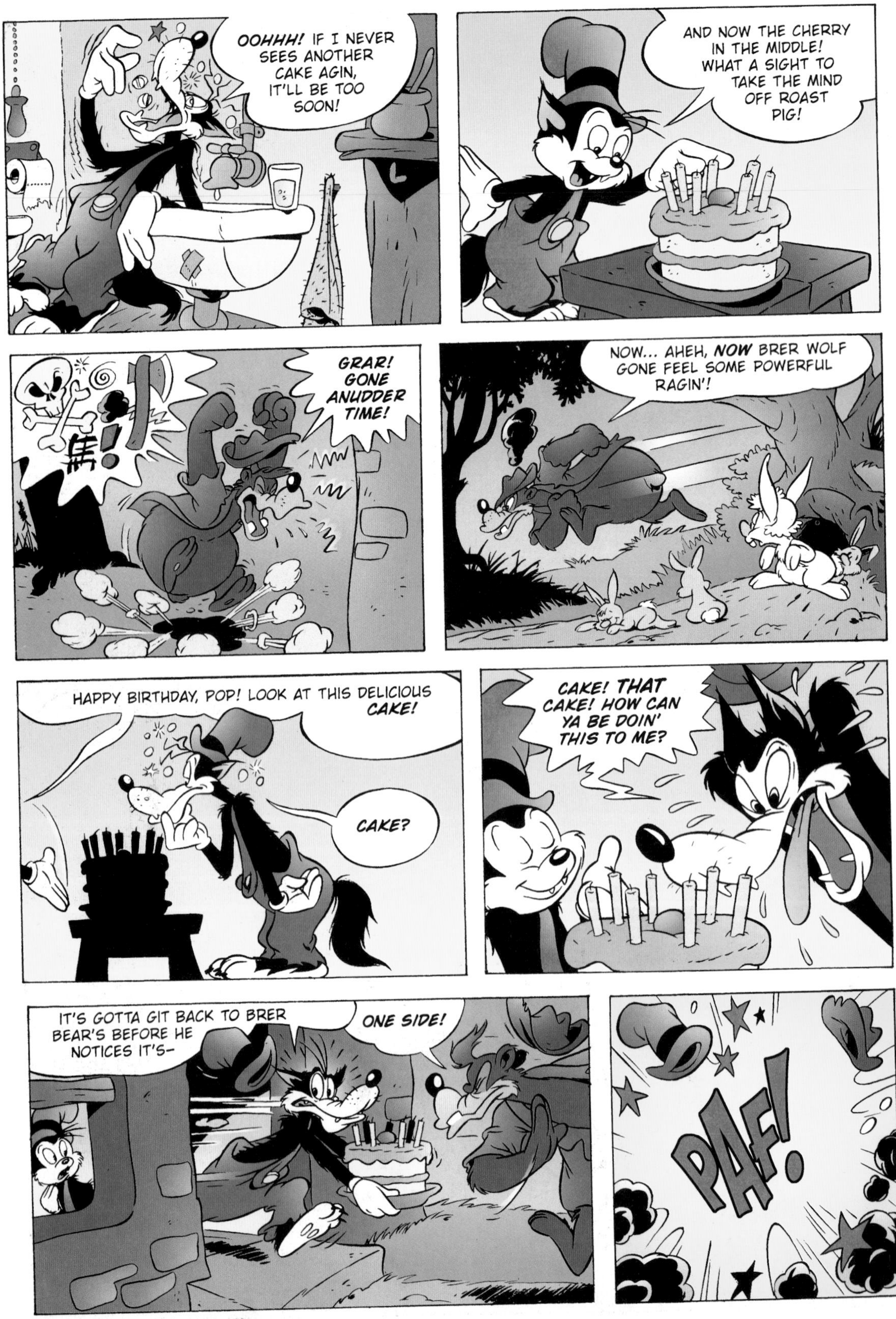
OOHHH! IF I NEVER SEES ANOTHER CAKE AGIN, IT'LL BE TOO SOON!
AND NOW THE CHERRY IN THE MIDDLE! WHAT A SIGHT TO TAKE THE MIND OFF ROAST PIG!
GRAR! GONE ANUDDER TIME!
NOW... AHEH, NOW BRER WOLF GONE FEEL SOME POWERFUL RAGIN'!
HAPPY BIRTHDAY, POP! LOOK AT THIS DELICIOUS CAKE!
CAKE?
CAKE! THAT CAKE! HOW CAN YA BE DOIN' THIS TO ME?
IT'S GOTTA GIT BACK TO BRER BEAR'S BEFORE HE NOTICES IT'S—
ONE SIDE!
PAF!

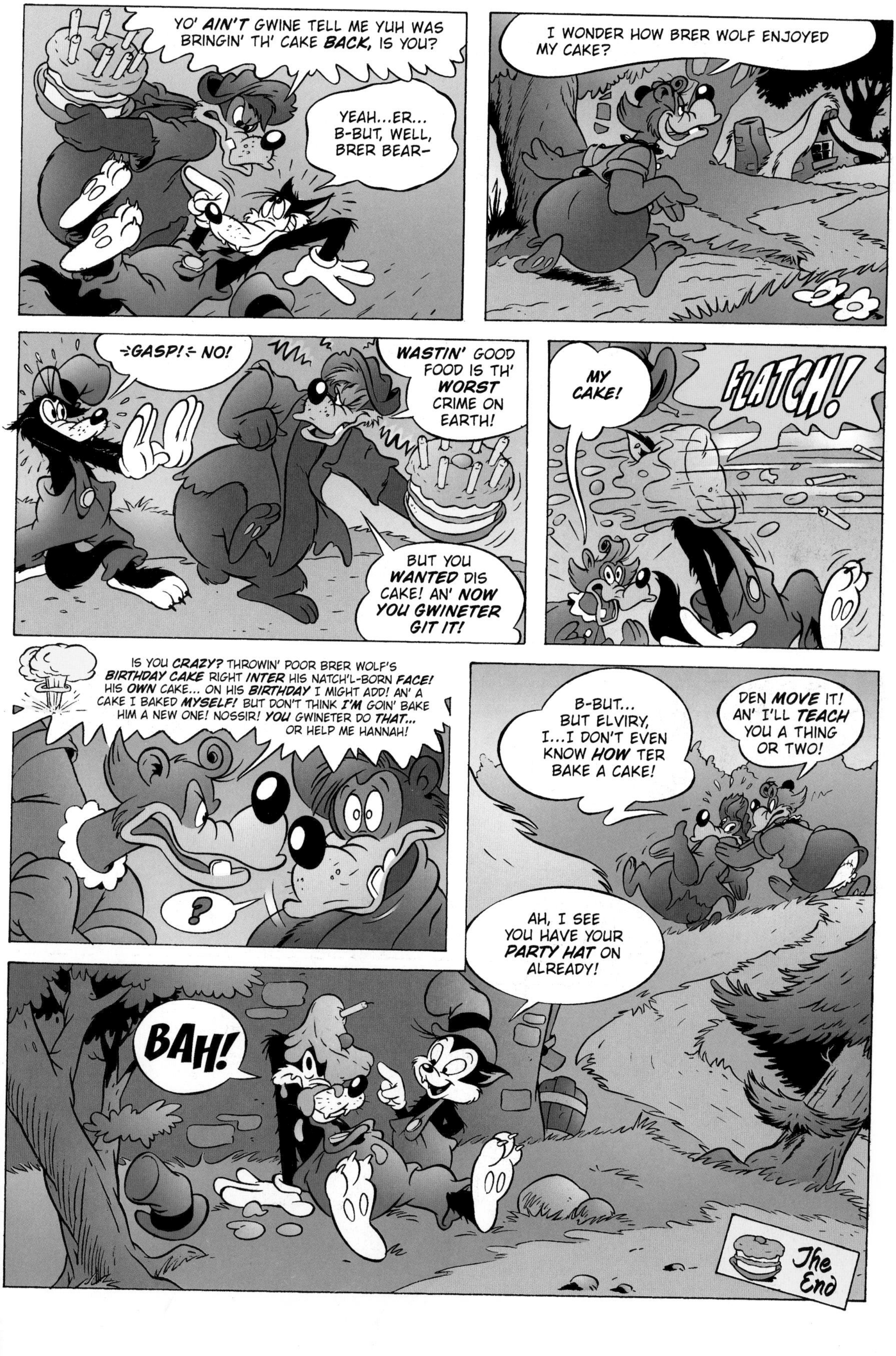
YO' AIN'T GWINE TELL ME YUH WAS BRINGIN' TH' CAKE BACK, IS YOU?
YEAH...ER... B-BUT, WELL, BRER BEAR–
I WONDER HOW BRER WOLF ENJOYED MY CAKE?
GASP! NO!
WASTIN' GOOD FOOD IS TH' WORST CRIME ON EARTH!
BUT YOU WANTED DIS CAKE! AN' NOW YOU GWINETER GIT IT!
MY CAKE!
FLATCH!
IS YOU CRAZY? THROWIN' POOR BRER WOLF'S BIRTHDAY CAKE RIGHT INTER HIS NATCH'L-BORN FACE! HIS OWN CAKE... ON HIS BIRTHDAY I MIGHT ADD! AN' A CAKE I BAKED MYSELF! BUT DON'T THINK I'M GOIN' BAKE HIM A NEW ONE! NOSSIR! YOU GWINETER DO THAT... OR HELP ME HANNAH!
?
B-BUT... BUT ELVIRY, I...I DON'T EVEN KNOW HOW TER BAKE A CAKE!
DEN MOVE IT! AN' I'LL TEACH YOU A THING OR TWO!
AH, I SEE YOU HAVE YOUR PARTY HAT ON ALREADY!
BAH!
The End

SUMMERTIME, LAZY RIVERS, HOUSEBOATS AND
SEA SERPENTS!!

When Donald and his nephews set sail on their new houseboat for fun and adventure, their voyage is riddled with mishaps, blunders, and foul-ups... would you expect anything less from Donald? But something beyond their wildest imaginations lurks beneath the lazy waters of the Ohio River, and as usual, it's up to the nephews to crack the case!

Ride along with the ducks in Carl Barks' classic adventure, "The Terror of the River!!" in *Vacation Parade 3,* Gemstone Publishing's fun-filled collection of summertime favorites! Available at your local comic shop in May, 2006.

This year's Summer spectacular also features the wrap-around cover from the original *Vacation Parade* 3, professionally restored by Rick Keene, as well as:

- A Don Rosa pin-up page of "Terror of the River!!"

- Mickey Mouse in "Sandgate," by Noel Van Horn

- Donald and Fethry in "The Fall Guy" by Dick Kinney and Al Hubbard

- "Goofy Gives His All" by Sarah Kinney and Rodriquez

- Pluto in "The-Not-So-Still Life," by Paul Murry (from *Walt Disney's Comics and Stories* 186)

- Li'l Bad Wolf in "Fooling the Fairy," by Gil Turner (from *Walt Disney's Comics and Stories* 102)

GEMSTONE PUBLISHING PRESENTS

WALT DISNEY'S
VACATION
PARADE
No. 3

$8.95

EEK!

GEMSTONE PUBLISHING

WWW.GEMSTONEPUB.COM/DISNEY

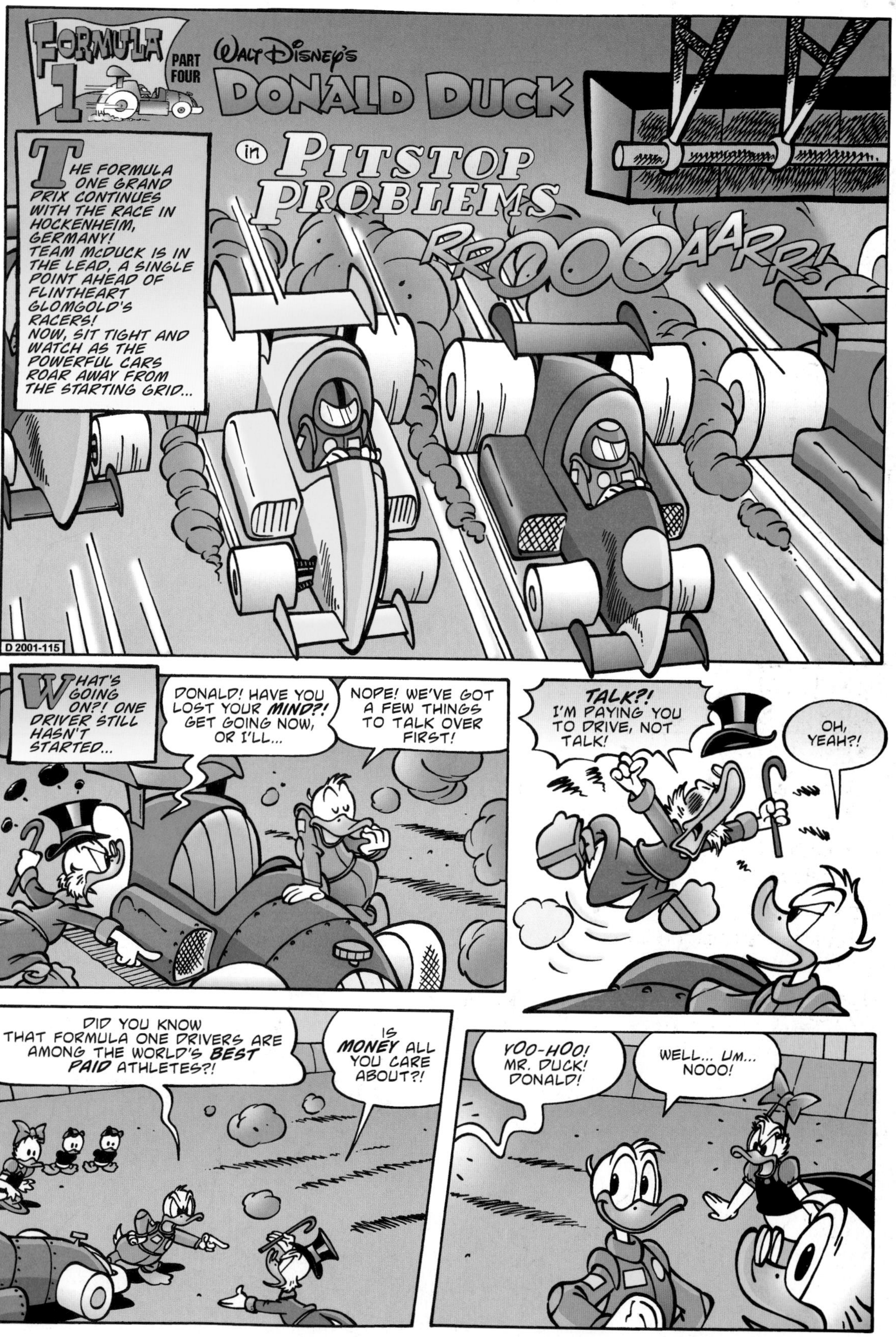
FORMULA 1
PART FOUR
WALT DISNEY'S
DONALD DUCK
in PITSTOP PROBLEMS
THE FORMULA ONE GRAND PRIX CONTINUES WITH THE RACE IN HOCKENHEIM, GERMANY! TEAM McDUCK IS IN THE LEAD, A SINGLE POINT AHEAD OF FLINTHEART GLOMGOLD'S RACERS! NOW, SIT TIGHT AND WATCH AS THE POWERFUL CARS ROAR AWAY FROM THE STARTING GRID...
RRROOOOAARR!
D 2001-115
WHAT'S GOING ON?! ONE DRIVER STILL HASN'T STARTED...
DONALD! HAVE YOU LOST YOUR MIND?! GET GOING NOW, OR I'LL...
NOPE! WE'VE GOT A FEW THINGS TO TALK OVER FIRST!
TALK?! I'M PAYING YOU TO DRIVE, NOT TALK!
OH, YEAH?!
DID YOU KNOW THAT FORMULA ONE DRIVERS ARE AMONG THE WORLD'S BEST PAID ATHLETES?!
IS MONEY ALL YOU CARE ABOUT?!
YOO-HOO! MR. DUCK! DONALD!
WELL... UM... NOOO!

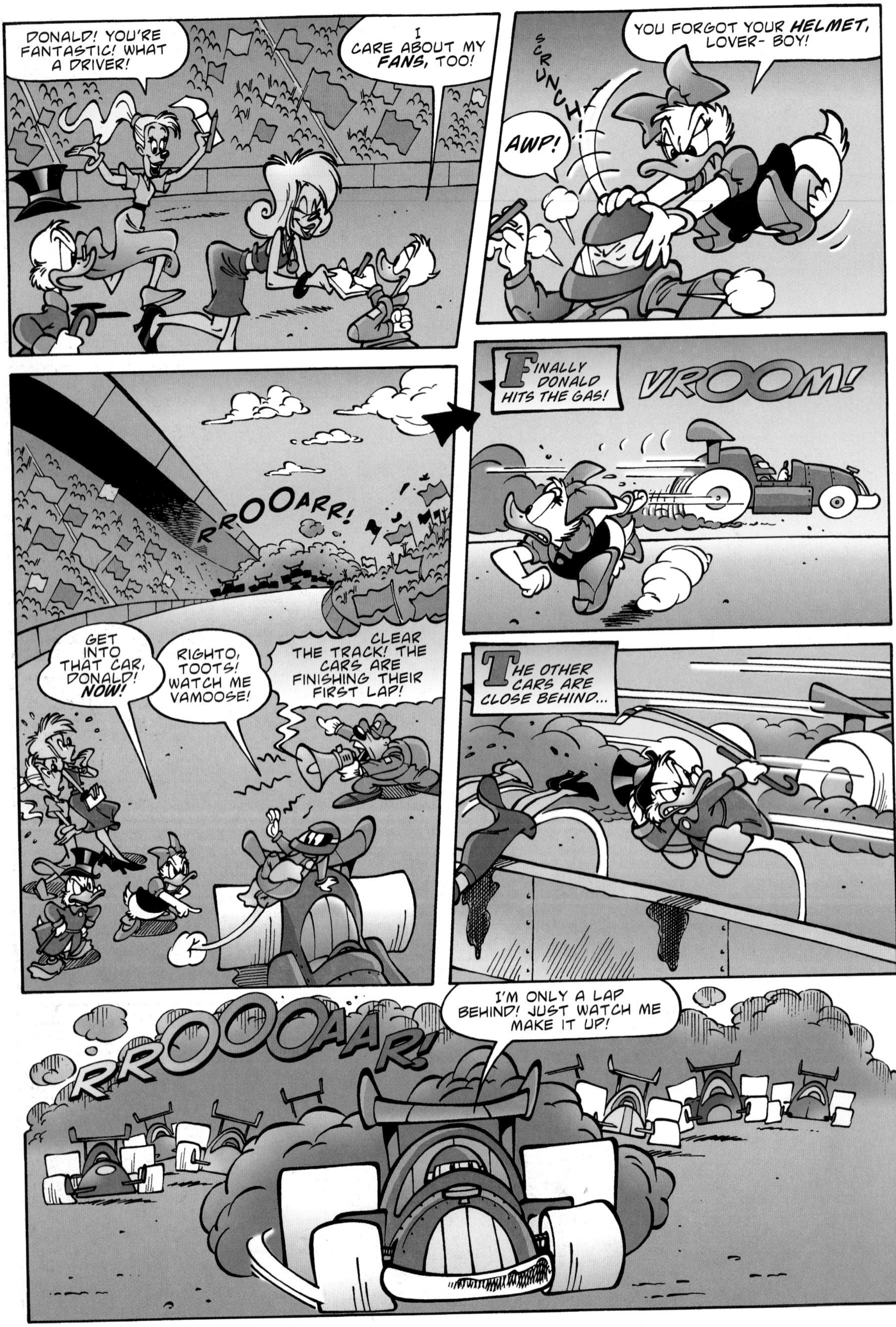
DONALD! YOU'RE FANTASTIC! WHAT A DRIVER!
I CARE ABOUT MY FANS, TOO!
SCRUNCH!
AWP!
YOU FORGOT YOUR HELMET, LOVER- BOY!
RROOARR!
GET INTO THAT CAR, DONALD! NOW!
RIGHTO, TOOTS! WATCH ME VAMOOSE!
CLEAR THE TRACK! THE CARS ARE FINISHING THEIR FIRST LAP!
FINALLY DONALD HITS THE GAS!
VROOM!
THE OTHER CARS ARE CLOSE BEHIND...
RROOOOAAR!
I'M ONLY A LAP BEHIND! JUST WATCH ME MAKE IT UP!

TO WIN UNCA DONALD'S GOING TO HAVE TO OUTDRIVE *UNCA DONALD!*

FORTUNATELY, I'VE SURPASSED MYSELF AS A MECHANIC! THAT CAR IS RUNNING FASTER TODAY THAN EVER!

UNFORTUNATELY, DONALD HAS SURPASSED *HIMSELF* AS A STUCK-UP MORON!

AND AS A MINDLESS, SKIRT-CHASING *FLIRT!*

GALL IN THE FAMILY, McDUCK?! HEH! HEH!

GRUMBLE!

YOU WOULDN'T *HAVE* THOSE PROBLEMS IF YOU HAD A TOP-NOTCH *PROFESSIONAL* TEAM!

SHUT YOUR BIG BEAK, GLOMGOLD!

WHOOSH!

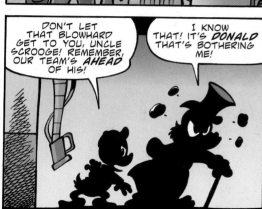

DON'T LET THAT BLOWHARD GET TO YOU, UNCLE SCROOGE! REMEMBER, OUR TEAM'S *AHEAD* OF HIS!

I KNOW THAT! IT'S *DONALD* THAT'S BOTHERING ME!

HE'S ACTING LIKE A BIG SHOT ALL OF A SUDDEN! DEMANDING MORE MONEY!

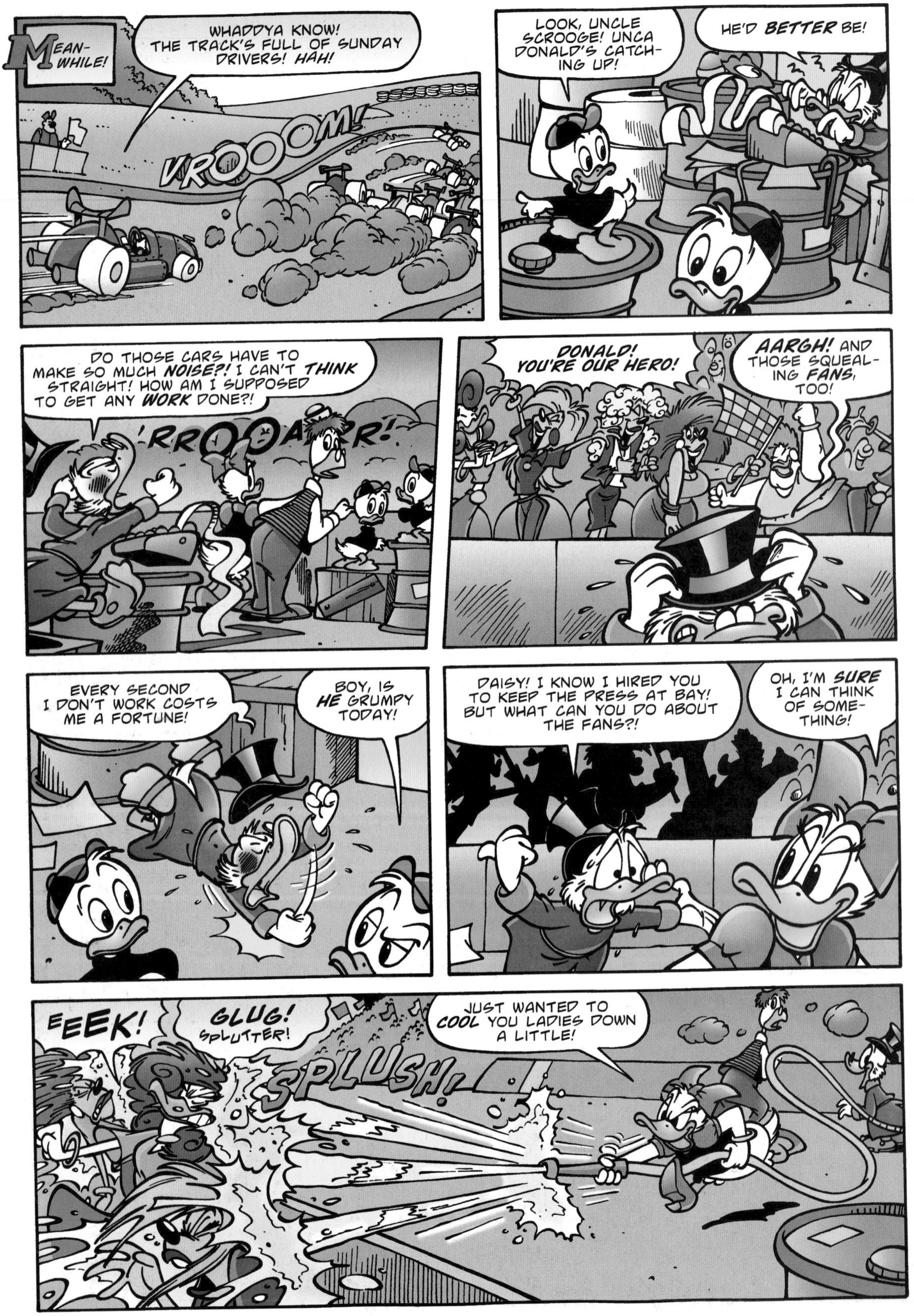
MEAN-WHILE!
WHADDYA KNOW! THE TRACK'S FULL OF SUNDAY DRIVERS! HAH!
VROOOOM!
LOOK, UNCLE SCROOGE! UNCA DONALD'S CATCHING UP!
HE'D BETTER BE!
DO THOSE CARS HAVE TO MAKE SO MUCH NOISE?! I CAN'T THINK STRAIGHT! HOW AM I SUPPOSED TO GET ANY WORK DONE?!
RROOAARR!
DONALD! YOU'RE OUR HERO!
AARGH! AND THOSE SQUEALING FANS, TOO!
EVERY SECOND I DON'T WORK COSTS ME A FORTUNE!
BOY, IS HE GRUMPY TODAY!
DAISY! I KNOW I HIRED YOU TO KEEP THE PRESS AT BAY! BUT WHAT CAN YOU DO ABOUT THE FANS?!
OH, I'M SURE I CAN THINK OF SOMETHING!
EEEK!
GLUG! SPLUTTER!
JUST WANTED TO COOL YOU LADIES DOWN A LITTLE!
SPLUSH!

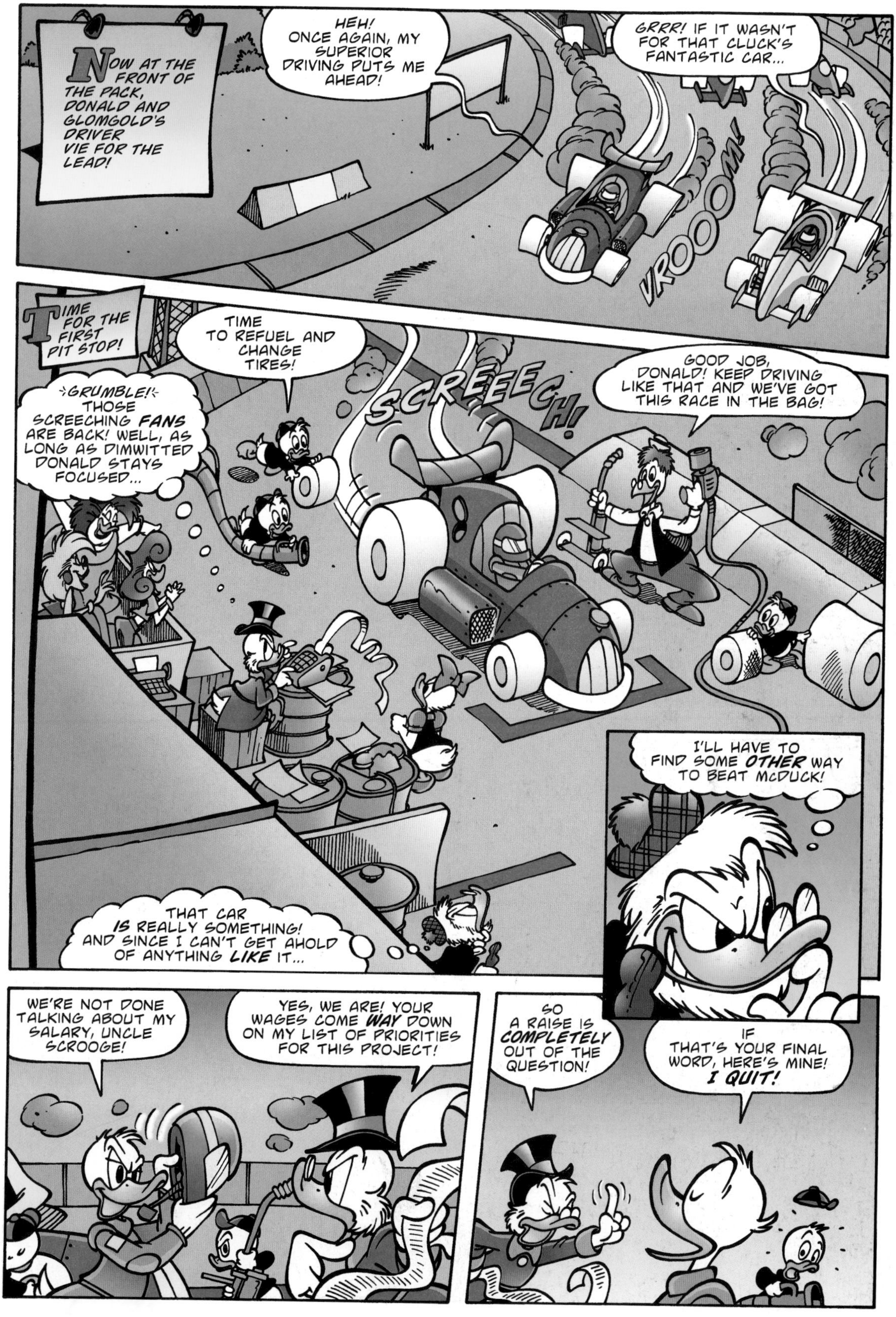
NOW AT THE FRONT OF THE PACK, DONALD AND GLOMGOLD'S DRIVER VIE FOR THE LEAD!
HEH! ONCE AGAIN, MY SUPERIOR DRIVING PUTS ME AHEAD!
GRRR! IF IT WASN'T FOR THAT CLUCK'S FANTASTIC CAR...
VROOOOM!
TIME FOR THE FIRST PIT STOP!
TIME TO REFUEL AND CHANGE TIRES!
SCREEECH!
GOOD JOB, DONALD! KEEP DRIVING LIKE THAT AND WE'VE GOT THIS RACE IN THE BAG!
GRUMBLE! THOSE SCREECHING FANS ARE BACK! WELL, AS LONG AS DIMWITTED DONALD STAYS FOCUSED...
THAT CAR IS REALLY SOMETHING! AND SINCE I CAN'T GET AHOLD OF ANYTHING LIKE IT...
I'LL HAVE TO FIND SOME OTHER WAY TO BEAT McDUCK!
WE'RE NOT DONE TALKING ABOUT MY SALARY, UNCLE SCROOGE!
YES, WE ARE! YOUR WAGES COME WAY DOWN ON MY LIST OF PRIORITIES FOR THIS PROJECT!
SO A RAISE IS COMPLETELY OUT OF THE QUESTION!
IF THAT'S YOUR FINAL WORD, HERE'S MINE! I QUIT!

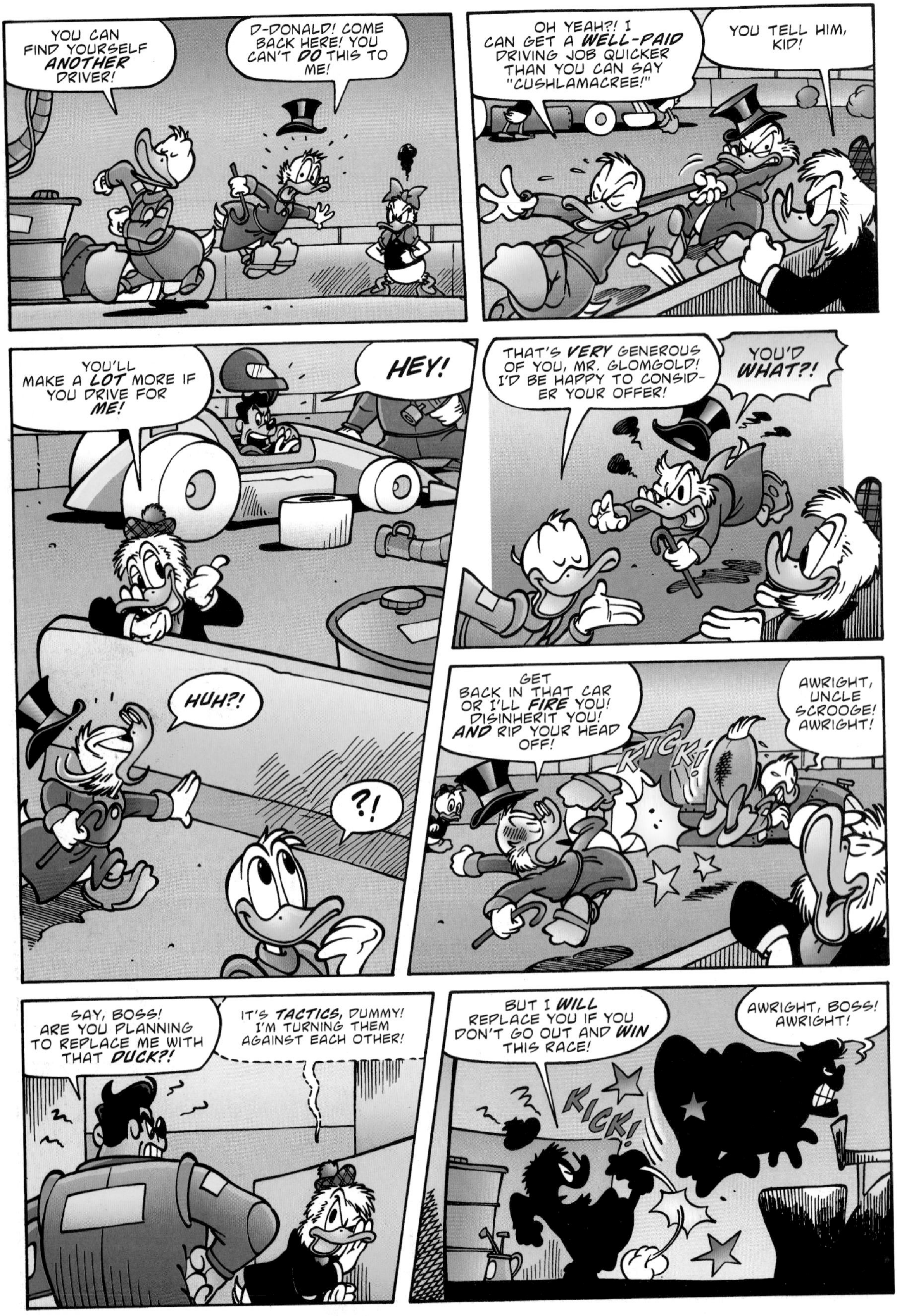
YOU CAN FIND YOURSELF ANOTHER DRIVER!
D-DONALD! COME BACK HERE! YOU CAN'T DO THIS TO ME!
OH YEAH?! I CAN GET A WELL-PAID DRIVING JOB QUICKER THAN YOU CAN SAY "CUSHLAMACREE!"
YOU TELL HIM, KID!
YOU'LL MAKE A LOT MORE IF YOU DRIVE FOR ME!
HEY!
HUH?!
?!
THAT'S VERY GENEROUS OF YOU, MR. GLOMGOLD! I'D BE HAPPY TO CONSIDER YOUR OFFER!
YOU'D WHAT?!
GET BACK IN THAT CAR OR I'LL FIRE YOU! DISINHERIT YOU! AND RIP YOUR HEAD OFF!
KICK!
AWRIGHT, UNCLE SCROOGE! AWRIGHT!
SAY, BOSS! ARE YOU PLANNING TO REPLACE ME WITH THAT DUCK?!
IT'S TACTICS, DUMMY! I'M TURNING THEM AGAINST EACH OTHER!
BUT I WILL REPLACE YOU IF YOU DON'T GO OUT AND WIN THIS RACE!
AWRIGHT, BOSS! AWRIGHT!
KICK!

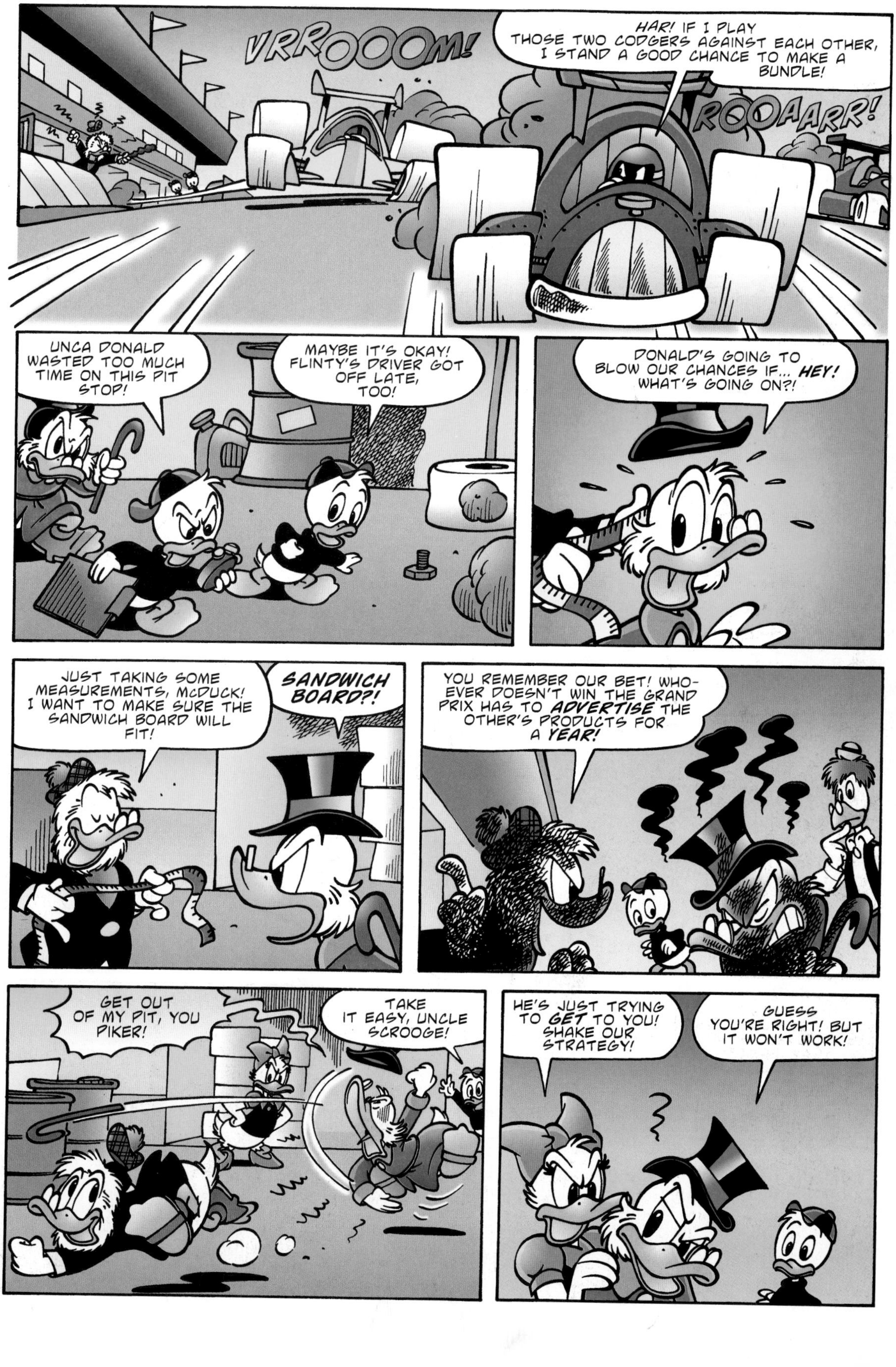

VRROOOM!
HAR! IF I PLAY THOSE TWO CODGERS AGAINST EACH OTHER, I STAND A GOOD CHANCE TO MAKE A BUNDLE!
ROOAARR!
UNCA DONALD WASTED TOO MUCH TIME ON THIS PIT STOP!
MAYBE IT'S OKAY! FLINTY'S DRIVER GOT OFF LATE, TOO!
DONALD'S GOING TO BLOW OUR CHANCES IF... HEY! WHAT'S GOING ON?!
JUST TAKING SOME MEASUREMENTS, McDUCK! I WANT TO MAKE SURE THE SANDWICH BOARD WILL FIT!
SANDWICH BOARD?!
YOU REMEMBER OUR BET! WHO-EVER DOESN'T WIN THE GRAND PRIX HAS TO ADVERTISE THE OTHER'S PRODUCTS FOR A YEAR!
GET OUT OF MY PIT, YOU PIKER!
TAKE IT EASY, UNCLE SCROOGE!
HE'S JUST TRYING TO GET TO YOU! SHAKE OUR STRATEGY!
GUESS YOU'RE RIGHT! BUT IT WON'T WORK!

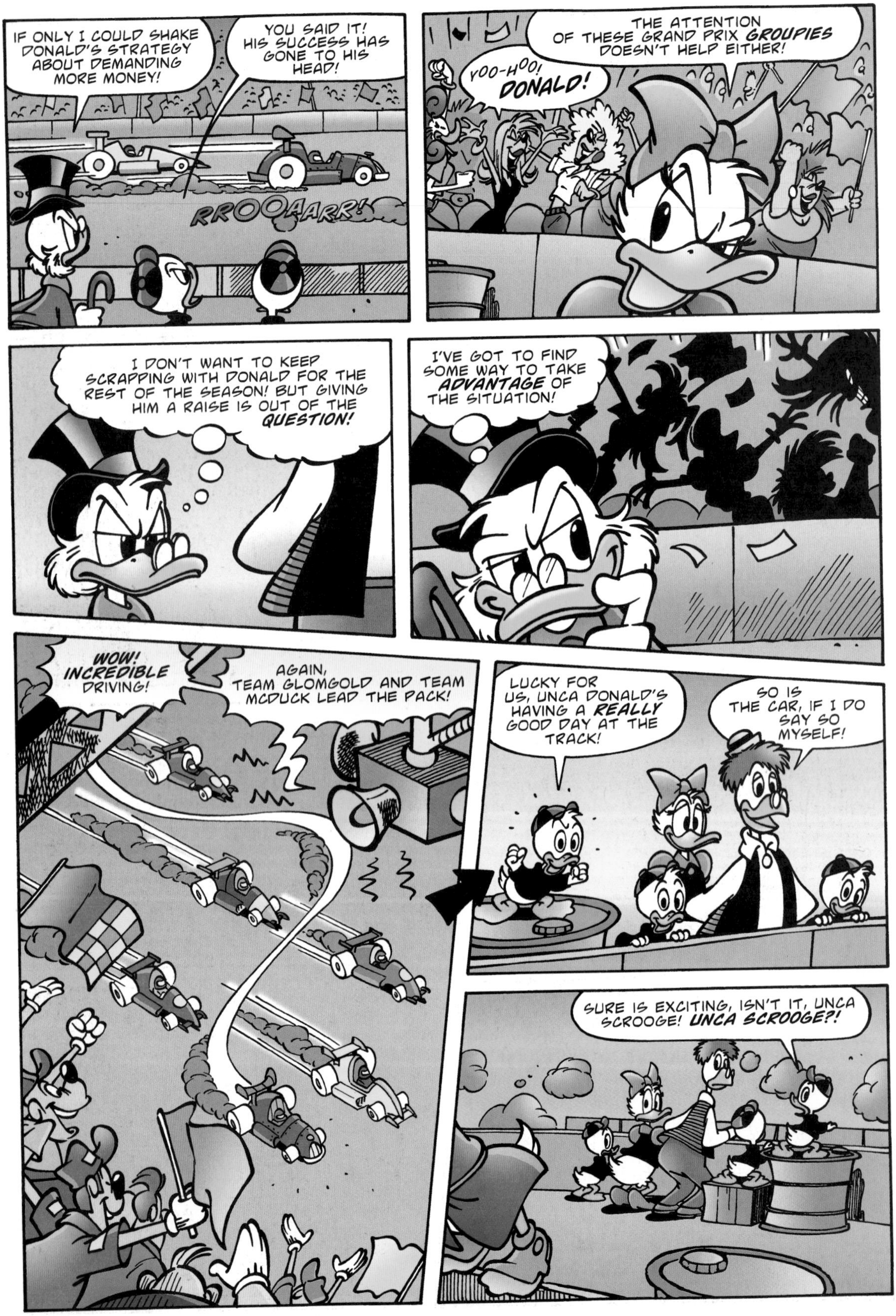
IF ONLY I COULD SHAKE DONALD'S STRATEGY ABOUT DEMANDING MORE MONEY!
YOU SAID IT! HIS SUCCESS HAS GONE TO HIS HEAD!
RROOAARR!
THE ATTENTION OF THESE GRAND PRIX GROUPIES DOESN'T HELP EITHER!
YOO-HOO! DONALD!
I DON'T WANT TO KEEP SCRAPPING WITH DONALD FOR THE REST OF THE SEASON! BUT GIVING HIM A RAISE IS OUT OF THE QUESTION!
I'VE GOT TO FIND SOME WAY TO TAKE ADVANTAGE OF THE SITUATION!
WOW! INCREDIBLE DRIVING!
AGAIN, TEAM GLOMGOLD AND TEAM MCDUCK LEAD THE PACK!
LUCKY FOR US, UNCA DONALD'S HAVING A REALLY GOOD DAY AT THE TRACK!
SO IS THE CAR, IF I DO SAY SO MYSELF!
SURE IS EXCITING, ISN'T IT, UNCA SCROOGE! UNCA SCROOGE?!

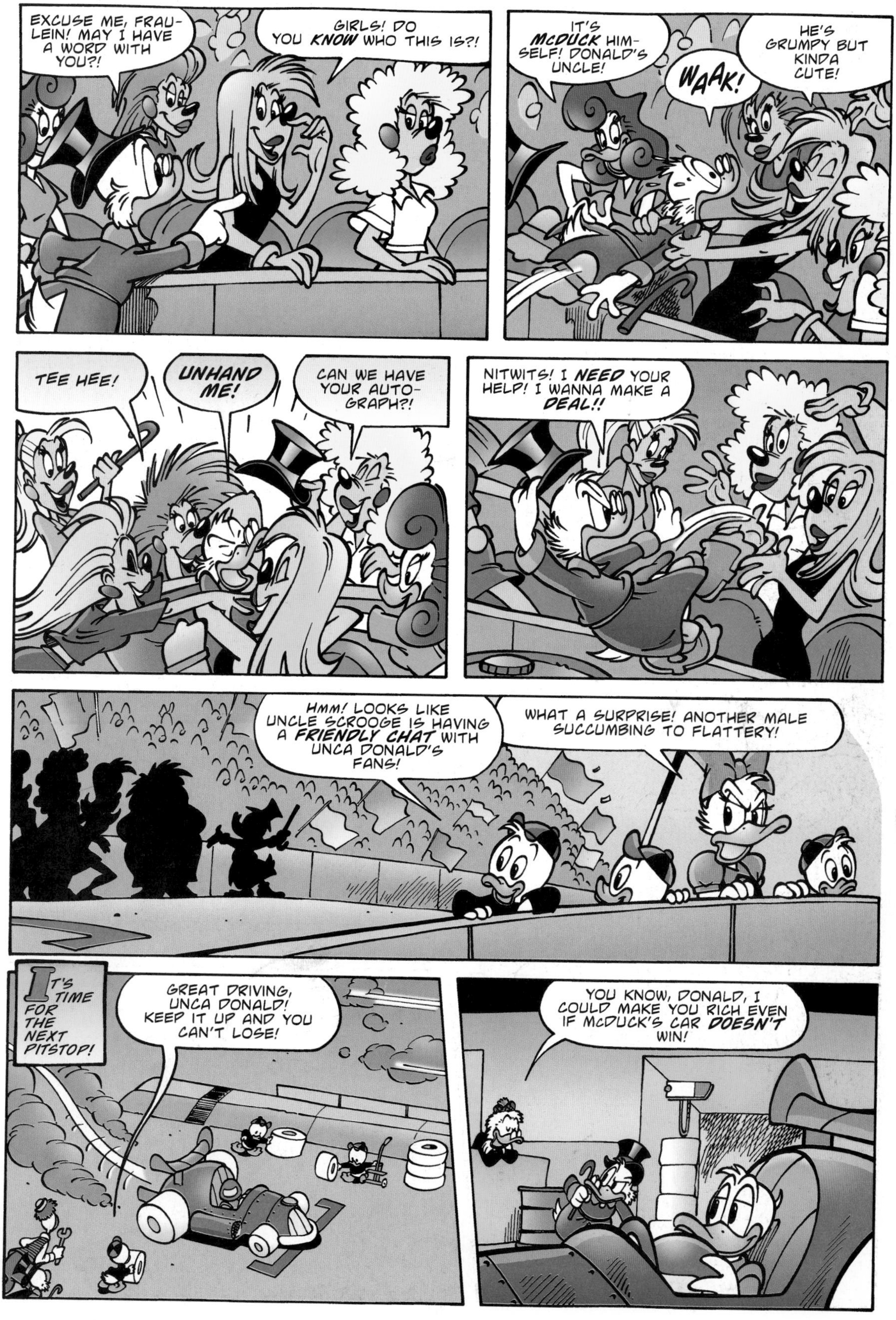
EXCUSE ME, FRAULEIN! MAY I HAVE A WORD WITH YOU?!
GIRLS! DO YOU KNOW WHO THIS IS?!
IT'S McDUCK HIMSELF! DONALD'S UNCLE!
WAAK!
HE'S GRUMPY BUT KINDA CUTE!
TEE HEE!
UNHAND ME!
CAN WE HAVE YOUR AUTOGRAPH?!
NITWITS! I NEED YOUR HELP! I WANNA MAKE A DEAL!!
HMM! LOOKS LIKE UNCLE SCROOGE IS HAVING A FRIENDLY CHAT WITH UNCA DONALD'S FANS!
WHAT A SURPRISE! ANOTHER MALE SUCCUMBING TO FLATTERY!
IT'S TIME FOR THE NEXT PITSTOP!
GREAT DRIVING, UNCA DONALD! KEEP IT UP AND YOU CAN'T LOSE!
YOU KNOW, DONALD, I COULD MAKE YOU RICH EVEN IF McDUCK'S CAR DOESN'T WIN!

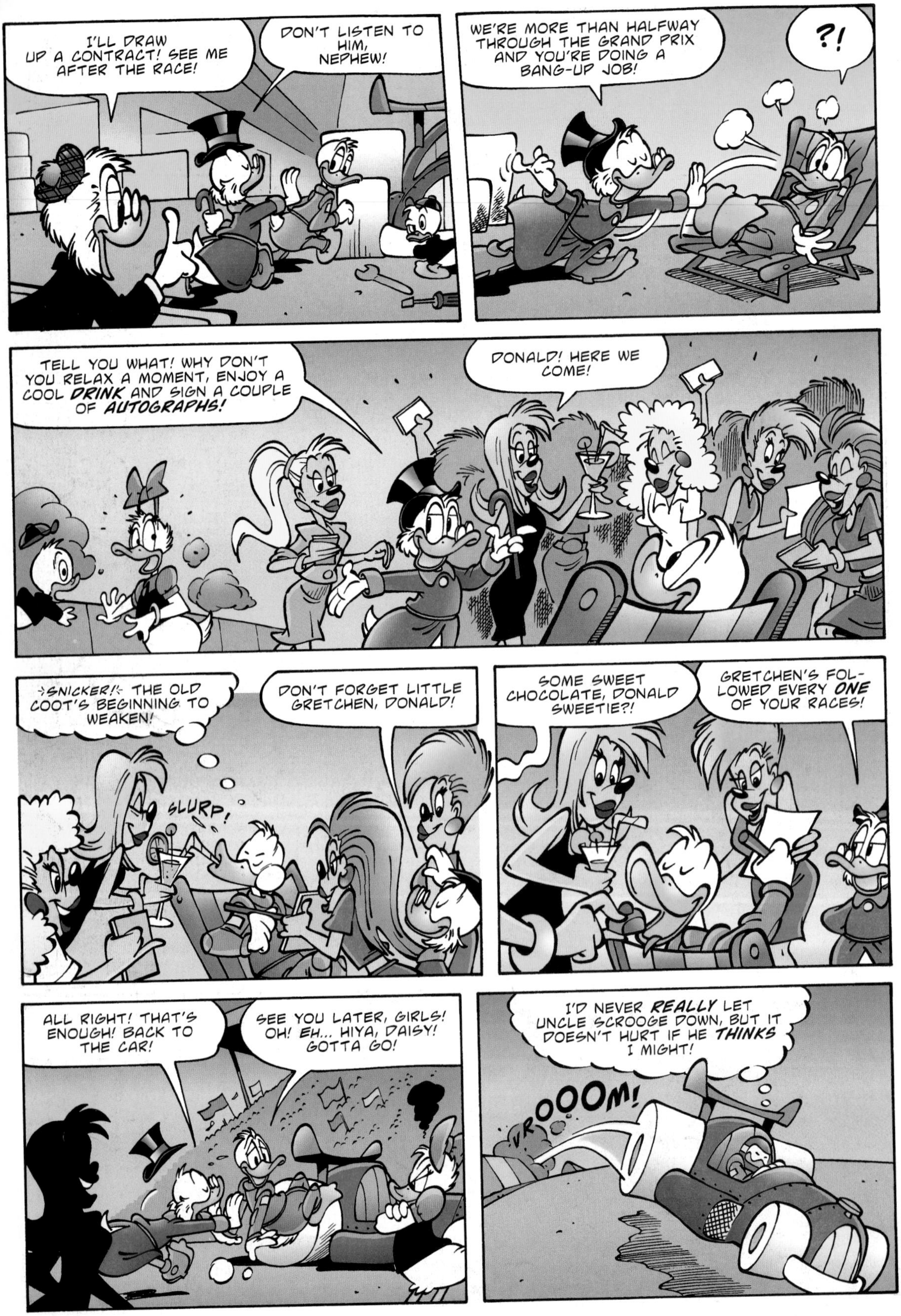
I'LL DRAW UP A CONTRACT! SEE ME AFTER THE RACE!
DON'T LISTEN TO HIM, NEPHEW!
WE'RE MORE THAN HALFWAY THROUGH THE GRAND PRIX AND YOU'RE DOING A BANG-UP JOB!
?!
TELL YOU WHAT! WHY DON'T YOU RELAX A MOMENT, ENJOY A COOL DRINK AND SIGN A COUPLE OF AUTOGRAPHS!
DONALD! HERE WE COME!
SNICKER! THE OLD COOT'S BEGINNING TO WEAKEN!
SLURP!
DON'T FORGET LITTLE GRETCHEN, DONALD!
SOME SWEET CHOCOLATE, DONALD SWEETIE?!
GRETCHEN'S FOLLOWED EVERY ONE OF YOUR RACES!
ALL RIGHT! THAT'S ENOUGH! BACK TO THE CAR!
SEE YOU LATER, GIRLS! OH! EH... HIYA, DAISY! GOTTA GO!
I'D NEVER REALLY LET UNCLE SCROOGE DOWN, BUT IT DOESN'T HURT IF HE THINKS I MIGHT!
VROOOOM!

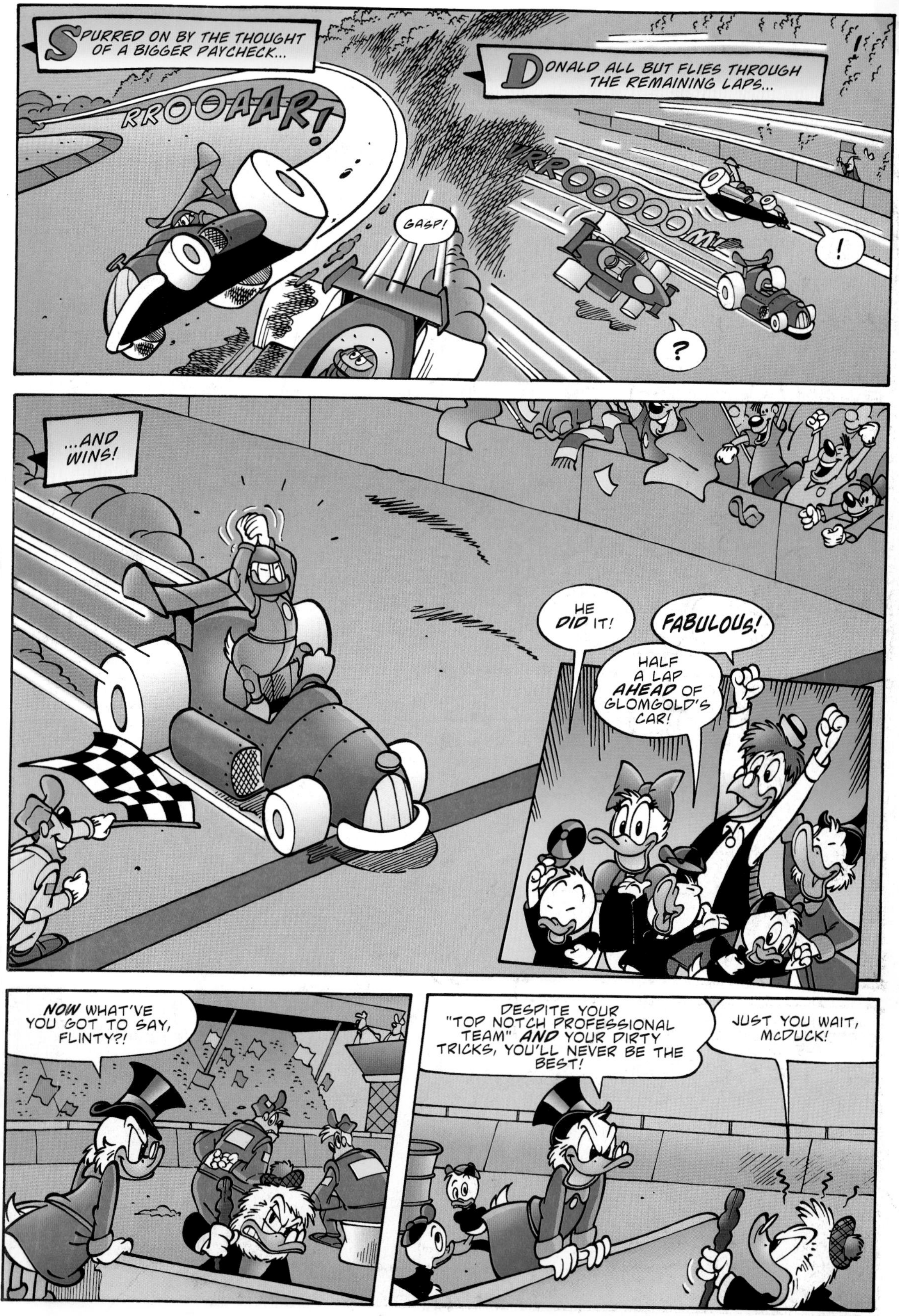
SPURRED ON BY THE THOUGHT OF A BIGGER PAYCHECK...
RROOAAR!
DONALD ALL BUT FLIES THROUGH THE REMAINING LAPS...
GASP!
VRROOOOOOM!
!
?
...AND WINS!
HE DID IT!
FABULOUS!
HALF A LAP AHEAD OF GLOMGOLD'S CAR!
NOW WHAT'VE YOU GOT TO SAY, FLINTY?!
DESPITE YOUR "TOP NOTCH PROFESSIONAL TEAM" AND YOUR DIRTY TRICKS, YOU'LL NEVER BE THE BEST!
JUST YOU WAIT, McDUCK!

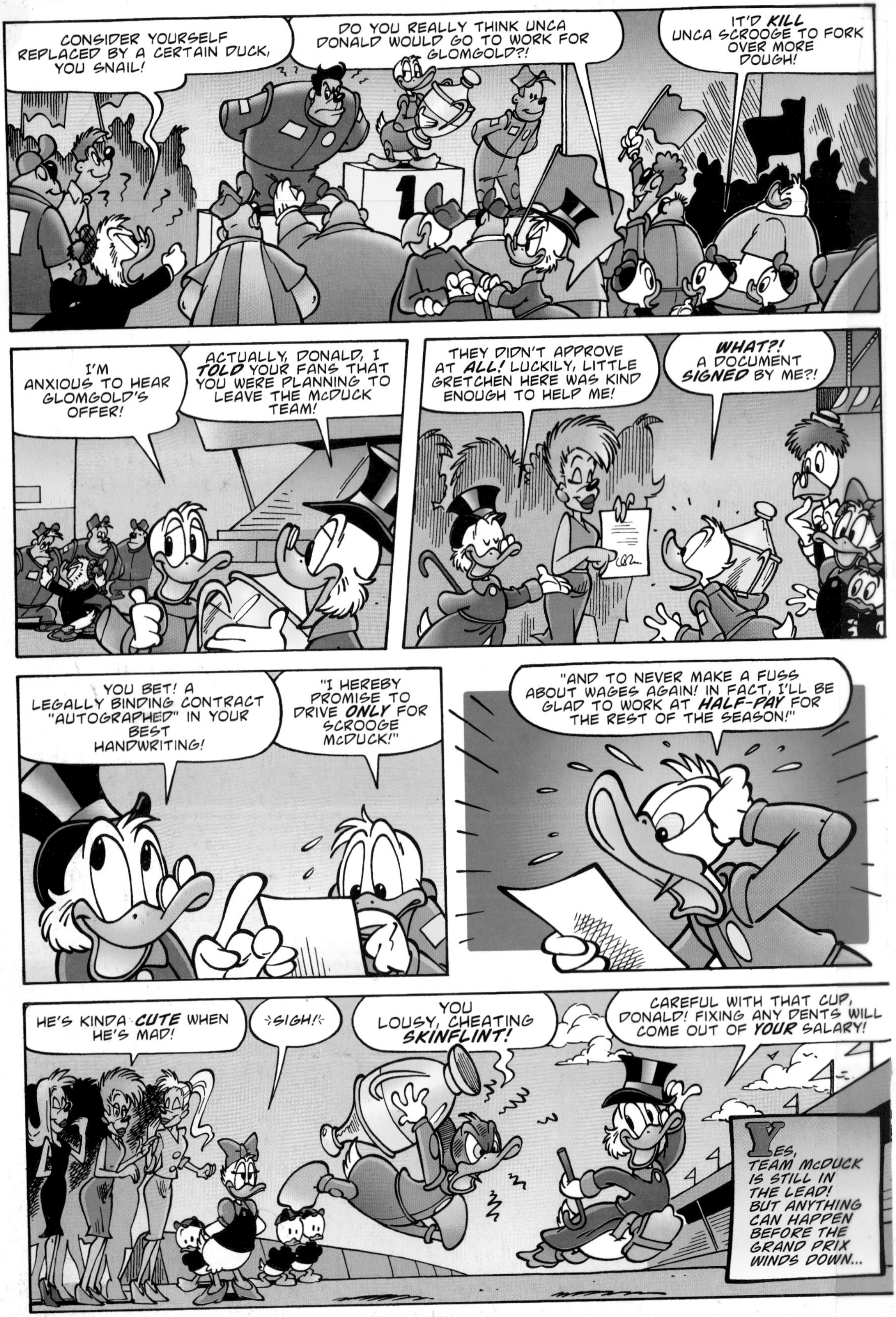
CONSIDER YOURSELF REPLACED BY A CERTAIN DUCK, YOU SNAIL!
DO YOU REALLY THINK UNCA DONALD WOULD GO TO WORK FOR GLOMGOLD?!
IT'D KILL UNCA SCROOGE TO FORK OVER MORE DOUGH!
I'M ANXIOUS TO HEAR GLOMGOLD'S OFFER!
ACTUALLY, DONALD, I TOLD YOUR FANS THAT YOU WERE PLANNING TO LEAVE THE McDUCK TEAM!
THEY DIDN'T APPROVE AT ALL! LUCKILY, LITTLE GRETCHEN HERE WAS KIND ENOUGH TO HELP ME!
WHAT?! A DOCUMENT SIGNED BY ME?!
YOU BET! A LEGALLY BINDING CONTRACT "AUTOGRAPHED" IN YOUR BEST HANDWRITING!
"I HEREBY PROMISE TO DRIVE ONLY FOR SCROOGE McDUCK!"
"AND TO NEVER MAKE A FUSS ABOUT WAGES AGAIN! IN FACT, I'LL BE GLAD TO WORK AT HALF-PAY FOR THE REST OF THE SEASON!"
HE'S KINDA CUTE WHEN HE'S MAD!
SIGH!
YOU LOUSY, CHEATING SKINFLINT!
CAREFUL WITH THAT CUP, DONALD! FIXING ANY DENTS WILL COME OUT OF YOUR SALARY!
YES, TEAM McDUCK IS STILL IN THE LEAD! BUT ANYTHING CAN HAPPEN BEFORE THE GRAND PRIX WINDS DOWN...